Survi

♡ xx

CONTENTS

Dedication
Prologue
Chapter One
Chapter Two
Chapter Three
Chapter Four
Chapter Five
Chapter Six
Chapter Seven
Chapter Eight
Chapter Nine
Chapter Ten
Chapter Eleven
Chapter Twelve
Chapter Thirteen
Chapter Fourteen
Chapter Fifteen
Chapter Sixteen
Chapter Seventeen
Chapter Eighteen
Chapter Nineteen
Chapter Twently
Chapter Twenty-One
Chapter Twenty-Two
Chapter Twenty-Three

Chapter Twenty-Four
Chapter Twenty-Five
Chapter Twenty-Six
Chapter Twenty-Seven
Chapter Twenty-Eight
Chapter Twenty-Nine
Chapter Thirty
Chapter Thirty-One
Chapter Thirty-Two
Chapter Thirty-Three
Chapter Thirty-Four
Chapter Thirty-Five
Chapter Thirty-Six
Epilogue
Note To Reader
Acknowledgements
Playlist
About The Author
Other Books

Surviving You

Dawn A Keane

Copyright 2015 Dawn Keane All rights reserved. The right of Dawn Keane to be identified as the author of the work has been asserted by her in accordance with the Copyright, Designs and Patents Act 1988.

All rights reserved. No part of this publication may be reproduced, stored in a retrieval system, or transmitted, in any form or by any means without the prior written consent of the publisher. Nor be otherwise circulated in any form of binding or cover other than that in which it is published and without a similar condition being imposed on the subsequent purchaser. All characters in this publication are fictional, and any resemblance to real persons, living or dead is purely coincidental.

DEDICATION

For my Uncle Ken, Johnny Lee Murphy and Karen. R.I.P My friends, the ones who believed in me; this is for you.

Dawn A Keane

"Thou shalt never be seen dead in white socks." "Thou shalt always drop our Hs."
"Thou shalt always respect three-quarter lengths or shorts even in winter." "Thou shalt always call our sibling our kid."
"Thou shalt always be mad for it." "Thou shalt always respect our elders."
"Thou shalt always be buzzing when happy."
"Thou shalt always work hard, play hard, fuck hard."
"Thou shalt never mither anyone for anything."
"Thou shalt never leave the house without carrying a gun, mobile phone, gloves and a balaclava."
"Thou shalt always protect the family."
"Thou shalt take the boy out of Manchester, but you cannot take Manchester out of the boy."

Dawn A Keane

PROLOGUE

TWELVE YEARS EARLIER

I drain the cold liquid from my glass and tip the remaining ice cubes into the wastebasket. Placing the glass against my bedroom wall, I listen closely to the loud noises coming from the next door neighbour's bedroom. My lungs begin to fill with much-needed air, the muffled ringing in my ears beginning to dull. Closing my eyes as tight as they can go, I gasp, trying to control my breathing, not wanting to make a single sound. My heartbeat thunders a hundred miles per hour inside my chest, and I attempt to slow it with deep, calming breaths. I cover my other ear with my free hand in hopes that the sounds will come through the glass pressed against the door a little clearer.

It sounds like people are shouting; a woman and a man, maybe. They're arguing about something, screaming at the top of their lungs. She's crying now, hiccupping with each sob. I can't hear anyone else in the room with them, just those two unfamiliar voices.

Standing here on the chair in my pink nightgown in the dark, I see him: a boy standing against his window. I jump with fear, startled. What is he doing? I move my head closer, squinting my eyes together. He's crying. I think he is hurt in some way. I can see his hands; his palms are flat against the window pane. The tears are streaming down his face, soaking his cheeks like the heavens have just opened and poured down around him.

I step off the chair slowly, not taking my eyes off this boy whose skin is stained with blood and tears. Placing my glass on the nightstand, I move slowly over to the window to get a closer look. I want to go to him, ask him why he is in so much pain, but I don't want to scare him. A dull ache settles in my chest—my heart hurts for him. As I lean against the cold glass, my heart breaks a little bit more. I watch hopelessly as his pain unfolds in front of my eyes. Each tear falling from his beautiful, dark eyes pierces my heart, sending a wave of pain through me. I press my palms and cheek against the glass, my breath steaming up the window.

I want to help him. He might be hurt.

Someone else might be hurt.

But I can't do anything but reach out to him. I push from the window with my hands—my back hitting the wall to the side of me—and slide slowly down the wall to the floor while my eyes remain glued to the figure before me. Tears roll down my cheeks, my own fear matching the beautiful boy.

ONE

Lee

My name is Lee Young. I can either be your best friend or your worst nightmare.

What a complete useless tosser. This guy is playing me, fucking with me yet again. And he knows exactly what he's doing. Wrong move, motherfucker. All he had to do was sort out the location for the drop. I asked him to do one thing. One fucking damn thing and he completely fucks it up, leaving me to find a new location. Dumb little fuck.

I want this done and dusted. It is one of my last jobs. This job and the one that will set me up financially for years to come will get my sister and me the fuck out of this gangster shit lifestyle we were born into living.

"Fuck it, Liam, I'll do it myself," I scowl through the phone, my tone sharp and short.

"Lee, man, let me sort this shit out for you. I can do it, mate. Just give me another chance, please? I'm begging you," Liam answers in his shaky, nervous, annoying-as-fuck voice. He sniffs inwardly through his nose, like his nostrils are packed full of shit, which only serves to piss me right off even more.

Running my hand through my hair, I rest it on the back of my neck in an attempt to soothe the blood threatening to boil up inside of me and spill out in frustration. I force the air into my lungs and close my eyes, taking deep, controlled breaths.

"No, Liam, this was your last chance. You're fucking done, you get me? Done." Slamming my phone down on the passenger seat with more force than I intended, it bounces off the windscreen and onto the floor. I find my eyes now staring back at me in the rear-view mirror—scowling dark brown, rimmed with thick black lashes. Lines crease between my eyes as my anger increases.

Turning toward the steering wheel, my hands grip the red and black leather tightly. Everything about this car sends tingles up and down my spine and calms my ever-growing anger. The leather bucket seats, interior, exterior, shiny black bodywork—if this car were a woman, she would be tanned right where she's parked.

I start up my Nissan Skyline and head out to call in well-overdue debts. My foot hits the pedal, turning onto the m62 and hoping to fuck no one gets in my way or gives me any more shit today. Fucking heads will roll. I arrive at Garthorpe Road in Wythenshawe, wanting to be anywhere else but in my hometown of Manchester. Parking the car up on the curb outside Smithy's hovel he calls a house

—I can't get my head around why he moved back in here when he had a shit hot apartment to live in. This shit hole belonged to his family—he grew up in it, he feels closer to the family that aren't around anymore. It used to be a home; warm and inviting. I used to go 'round for my tea as a really small child before his parents died, the smell of home-cooked food filled the place, and the fire was always lit. His mum kept ornaments all over the house horse and cart style, royal family cups and plates sat proudly in a glass and wooden cabinet. His mum would sit and play with us on the living room floor; Connect Four, Monopoly, you name it. She looked just like an angel, his mum did, sent down from heaven and then she was gone and became one for real. Now the house is run-down, not an ornament or board game in sight. It is cold and badly in need of decorating. He has all the mod cons technology wise, but the house has lost that warmth of being a family home now; it's as if his parents were never here. Smithy's Aunt had moved in shortly after, but whatever family was left didn't have a lot to do with Smithy. He was 'round our house more often than not, and it was obvious losing his parents took

something from him; that light he had inside him snuffed out. For a long time, my dad tried to make sure he got some of that back.

I push my gun in the back of my jeans and jump out, slamming the car door behind me with more force than intended. I stalk toward his front door, cringing at the sound my car just made.

"All right, mate?" I greet a pale-faced, scruffy-looking Smithy standing in the doorway in nothing but a pair of black boxer briefs. His normally tanned skin is pastier than usual. He used to be built like a tank, but his once huge-muscled frame has turned to skin and bone. With a few days' worth of stubble on his chin, he looks like the cokehead he's turned into. Like the ghost of my old friend.

"All right, Lee, mate, how's things?" he asks.

"Calling all debts in, Smith. As in now." I look around the hovel he lives in, taking in the two half- naked bitches lying on the sofa.

They're all completely wasted on the coke they've sniffed up their noses, looking skanky as hell with just-fucked hair and smudged lipstick. The smell of sex permeates the air and condom wrappers are scattered on the floor around the room. I pick up some bits of clothes in front of my feet that I assume belong to them and launch them at the two women with a scowl on my face.

"I don't have the patience for this shit," I bellow at them. "Put some fucking clothes on, bitches." The blonde lifts her hands up in the air in a surrender gesture.

"OK, Mr. Angry." She laughs, smiling and staring at me like she wants to eat me. Aiming my death scowl at Smithy, he ushers both women into his bedroom as fast as he can move them.

My eyes take in everything around me. Lines of coke, a credit card, and a rolled up twenty lay out on the coffee table. Bags of drugs and a few empty ones litter the once nice-looking room. Empty beer bottles lie on the floor and vodka sits on the table. All of this out in the open for the whole fucking world to see. What the fuck is he playing at?
Smithy comes back into the living room dressed in a white tee and jeans. My dog, a black and white Staffordshire bull terrier called Sniper, runs on the treadmill in the corner of the room. He's breathing hard, his white teeth on show and pink tongue catching each of his breaths. Fuck, the dog's got more meat and muscle on him than Smithy. I walk over to him and kneel down to pat his head in greeting. Smithy has looked after him well for me; I'll give him that. Once I get my shit sorted, he's coming back to Scotland with me and out of this dump for good.
There was a time I would have gone right back to that bedroom with those two bitches as soon as I walked through the front door, fucking their brains out into the house next door, but not anymore. I don't have the time or space in my head for anyone right now. My thoughts are pre-occupied with a certain brunette that's currently a few hundred miles away anyhow. Women complicate things too much, and my life is far too complicated as it is.
"Fifty grand, Smith. I want it back yesterday, mate." I pin him with my scowl.

I've been mates with this guy since I was four years old; I do not want to beat him to death because of money. Or anything else, for that matter. He might have different parents, but he's my brother all the same.

"Calm the fuck down, Lee, mate. Seriously, you need anger fucking management."

He waves his hand toward the safe on the far wall and moves in that direction. I turn off the treadmill, releasing Sniper, who immediately jumps on me, forcing my ass to Smithy's sofa. He licks every part of my face he can get his tongue around, wagging his black tail a hundred miles an hour. Smithy takes out fifty grand and hands it over to me. Searching my face with a quizzical look, he asks, "Why now, mate? You in trouble?"

He searches my blank expression for an answer, but I close down any indication of why I'm calling everything in. I've learned never to show any sign of weakness, even to one of my oldest friends. My dad taught me well...among other things. I stand and move to walk out of the door. With the knob in my hand, I twist but turn back to Smithy before I leave.

"Just want what's mine. Put the word out, mate. I'll be in touch in a few days. And sort your shit out. This place is a fucking mess." Walking away with his eyes burning into my back, I reach my car and drive off, not looking back at the area my dad once ran like an army.

I stare at my reflection in the mirror, a bulletproof vest protecting my torso. Here's hoping they've got a shit aim, and I don't end up with a bullet in my brain. I checked into a hotel, a hotel that belongs to my father, so I can be in and out of this job and get to my uncle in record time. This life…It's like being a ghost, sweeping in and out of places undetected. I need to get out, I must get out of this life, I scream inside my head.

I run my hand over my Kevlar, double checking it's secure, checking I have everything I need. I slide on my black gloves and head out into the dimly-lit hallway. I scan it as I move seeing there's nobody around, thank fuck. The light bulb in the hall is flickering on and off. I must remember to tell my dad to fix that.

Making my way through the back exit fire door—careful not to let it slam shut—I head down to where I parked the car needed for this job. One I can burn after this is done. I drive to Holly-Hedge Road in Benchill; I got word that the guy we've been looking for will be at a garage there working late and alone. This motherfucker owes us money—a lot of money.

We did some digging, found out he's a fucking convicted pedophile, and they let the fucker out amongst kids; near schools and parks. I don't give a shit about the money. He's fucking dead.

The sound of the car door slamming shut echoes around the garage walls. Tucked behind the dark alleyway at the side, I watch him move around the car and wait silently for my chance. My skin is itching with need, to torture the fucker until he bleeds out. The clinking of another car door opening makes my heart race even faster. My knuckles crack with the intensity of my grip on my gun. I'm a fucking killer, a murderer, the monster that my dad has created. I don't want to be this man, but right now I want nothing more than to spill this evil monster's blood.

I slide my back against the wall as silently as possible, keeping my eyes locked on to my target the whole time. He moves back to the engine of the car he's working on and leans in to take a look. I take my chance.

Coming up behind him, I reach my arm around his neck putting my gun between his legs, so it's wedged under his balls, and I fire the gun, letting his body slide to the floor. Easy.

My breathing becomes ragged. My bulging muscles cord with my effort to turn him around and face me. I need to kill. It is the only way to stop this rage deep inside me, to temper the constant haze of red—I need more blood.

I lift my arm without saying a single word and aim it at the dirty scum quivering and begging for his life on the garage floor. I pay him no mind, ignoring his pleas. It has to be done; I need to make it right and get some kind of justice for those kids he hurt. Just thinking about that makes the blood in my veins boil even more, so I fire again, this time right between the eyes, his blood spattering everywhere.

I growl to myself, "I'll do your job for you." I talk to myself or God, or the justice system, I'm not sure. Fire pulses through my veins with such intensity as the adrenaline takes over, that I start to move away from the body and into the dark shadows of the garage walls. Suddenly, I hear footsteps coming

toward the entrance of the garage, so I move quicker and head for the car, getting out of there as fast as my legs can carry me.

Two

Rose

As soon as we exit the police station, I rush over to Jane. "Congratulations!" She smiles and accepts my hug, her arms spread out wide. I hold her tightly in my arms, smiling as I do while she wraps her arms around me. It feels good.

I love my job. Behind the scenes of the café, Dana and I run a women's aid; a place women can come to. The café is a cover for what we really do. We set it up to help women like us, women like me. I suffered at the hands of my ex-boyfriend's brutal temper, and I didn't want to see others suffer the same.

Pulling back from Jane's hold, I place her hand in mine and admit, "It was my pleasure, sweet."

I run her through the plan of action as we walk the length of the car park. "So now that we have the interdict out on him, we have the law on your side, so he doesn't have a leg to stand on. Should give you some breathing space." I run my hand up her arm in a comforting gesture. "If he tries to contact you in any way, shape, or form, call the police, OK? Then you call me." I give her a pointed look, hoping she sees the sincerity.
Jane rolls her eyes at me. "Yes, I promise I will call them, and then I'll call you."

I chuckle because we have been through this before. It isn't even funny, not the reality of it, but Jane is only eighteen and thinks of me as being too overprotective. I like to make sure people have things in place to keep them safe from violent predators, from the nightmares that keep them awake at night. And stay that way. If I could find my ex, I would do the same, but it's like he never existed—he just disappeared off the face of the earth. I have been where Jane is now: scared out of my mind, looking over my shoulder every time I step out of my front door, panicked thoughts whirling inside my mind. I might be physically free of him now, but am I really? In my head, I'm not, and I wonder if I will ever be free of him. I still feel like I'm living like a prisoner, wondering if I am going to die today or the next day. At the hands of my ex-partner Mike. He was brutally wicked to me, punishing me for what, I still don't know. Tortured for not toeing the line like he felt I should have when I always tried to do everything his way. It was so exhausting. I don't think I was ever able to make him happy. I felt like I was walking on eggshells every minute of every day in an attempt to keep the peace so he didn't lose his temper with me or my daughter Annie.

I still live with that excruciating, terrifying fear after a year of being away from Manchester, a year of being away from him and his controlling ways. I had fled with my daughter to a women's refuge in the city, fleeing my home and my friends, well the few that I had. My job. My life. Everything that I knew, everything that was me. I had been treated so badly I knew that I had to leave him as soon as possible or one day I would be leaving my daughter without her mother. I had to get my baby girl and myself as far away from him as possible, just to be safe.

He had been out at work at a gig in one of the clubs, and I knew he would be getting high on whatever drugs he could get his hands on. He would be reeking of alcohol when he eventually strolled home. *I crawled my way through the gap into our attic to retrieve a few sentimental things like Annie's birth certificate and her baby photographs. I hated going up there; it was dark, dirty, and full of sharp nails that stuck out of the wood and scraped your skin. The useless old insulation made me claw at my skin for days. The oppression I felt in that attic with its dark and dusty corners echoed the shadows that surrounded my life. But I wasn't leaving those things behind because he would never hand them over to me willingly. Or let me go. I would be dragged home by my hair, kicking and screaming.*

When I got to the women's refuge, I sighed with relief at the thought that I had actually done it; I was finally free of him physically. It was the most amazing feeling in the world. I'm not a crier, but I cried a river of tears every night that I was safe in a strange bed cuddled into my boo. All of the pain and the feelings of dread, fear, and worthlessness worked its way through every pore, never fully leaving me. Mentally he was still there haunting my dreams and every decision I tried to make. He always had control of everything.

I still sleep with the light on at night. I keep my baseball bat beside my bed, knowing Mike is out there somewhere, lurking, probably watching and waiting to strike and pounce on his prey because let's face it, that's all I am to him - prey, his property. Not a human being with feelings. But what he doesn't realize is that this prey is stronger and wiser than she was before.

I set up the woman's aid when we opened up the café and offices soon after we moved to Jedburgh, because I feel so passionate and so deeply for the cause, the same way that Dana does. The effect our own experiences have had on us are still deeply entrenched within us in ways I'm sure one day will ease. Why should anyone have to live in fear of any man or any other person? Why should anyone feel so worthless and believe that they should have to live that way because they feel they don't deserve any better? Why should anyone walk on eggshells day in and day out scared out of their mind wondering if the person that claims to love you will beat you that night? Unable to have friends of your own for fear of what he might do to you, terrified that one of your children might hear something or get in the way of his attack and get hurt themselves. Fear of him turning on one of your children, unable to live a full and happy life. I will fight until I'm dead to keep my baby, myself, and anyone else I can safe. If all the work, we do helps someone else then it's all worthwhile; my job is done.

Smiling at Jane, I place my hand on her forearm and squeeze softly. "You know I'm always here for you, day or night, both Dana and I. Call us anytime, OK? Do you hear me?"

Jane wipes away a tear that has slipped down her cheek; maybe I wasn't the only one lost in painful memories.

"Thank you, Rose, for everything you have done for me. You have made my life worth living again. I cannot thank you enough for that."

Surviving You

Walking back toward my car feeling lighter on my feet than I did yesterday, knowing that Jane would most likely sleep a bit better tonight because she officially has the law on her side. It feels like a small celebration to some but for us it's huge. I tell Jane, "Anytime."

Three

Lee

My father; the serial killer King of the underground; the King and head of my family every fucker around the city was and still is terrified of. That burden was soon passed onto me when it was my turn to live up to my father's name—to be feared by many when I was old enough to handle it. I took over a few things in the business, but I fucking despise the life I grew up in with a passion. My heart beats like any other, but it became as black as coal only working for one purpose: keeping me alive. The area I grew up in—an area with so many great memories as an average everyday kid—housed distant memories tucked away in little boxes inside of my brain. Ever since I took on the role that was coveted by many, it changed my world forever. Prison life is shit, and I don't want to end up back in there, ever. It's not that I can't handle myself, I just can't stand having my freedom ripped away from me, caged like a bird that can't fly because its wings have no room to spread. Restricted. A limited amount of room to grow, to be free.

Surviving You

Moss Side looks a lot different now. All new builds right near the city center of Manchester are looking a lot nicer than the old, worn-out houses that stick out like a sore thumb. Yet behind those new walls, it's the same old shit from back then. They can change the area all they fucking want, but they can't change the people. Gun runners, drug dealers, pimps and junkies. Some of the worst cockroaches you will ever meet in your fucking life, and I have my Dad to thank for growing up with these ass wipes. He had to be a gang member, not a fucking accountant or a lawyer or just a regular Joe. A god damn gang member running alongside some of the most dangerous criminals ever to walk the streets of Manchester and the UK. He wanted the world at his feet, and he took Manchester like it was his God-given birth right. I was fucked from the day I was born, destined to be in this life whether I wanted it or not, and to one day take over from my Dad when the time came. That time came quicker than I expected.

I arrive at Claremont Road in Moss Side. I can hear Bob Marley wailing out of Uncle Mark's front door. He's in his chair on his front step like always. He tokes on a massive joint, the smolder rising from it in a two-toned puff of smoke, drifting up in the air just like always. Mark blows the smoke out of his mouth he had inhaled showing me his broad smile and perfect teeth as he stands and pulls me into a big man hug. There's comfort in the old man's arms.

"Lee, my boy, where've you been?" he asks, his whole face beaming with happiness as he passes the joint. I take it from him and inhale it deep into my lungs; it tastes and smells like fucking heaven in a cigarette paper. I close my eyes and savor the calm that it induces.

"Uncle Mark, this is the shit." And it is. Talk about blowing your mind.

"Only home-grown green shit, the best in this house, my boy, none of that stuff packed with chemicals." He smiles with a questioning look in his almost black eyes taking back his joint from me while Bob sings "Don't Worry, Be Happy" in the background. "You need anything, Lee? What brings you to this neck of the woods?" My uncle searches my face. He knows I need a favour, it must be written all over me, and he's one of the few people in my life I let read me. Let might be too strong a word; Mark's always been able to read every single thing before it's even past my lips.

"Liam fucked up the drop, and I need somewhere quick." My uncle's smile could not get any wider; he loves this shit. We have other people do most of the jobs these days, but my uncle likes to get his hands dirty still and enjoys stepping in with the major jobs; he misses being on the front line.

"Give me the details. It goes through me now, son, I'll get this done but you need to kick that guy's ass back into touch, Lee, weak links like him fall back on you. Trouble now is too many of the younger ones shoving too much shit up their noses to care about why they're in this. Those pricks wind up in prison for life or end up dead because they're too fucking stupid." Isn't that the truth?

"He's getting more and more paranoid and jittery by the second. Every time I see him it's worse than the last. I'm cutting everyone loose, calling in all debts. I want out, Mark; it's time." I pause for a moment to make sure he gets that I'm serious. "I've got a couple of big properties in Scotland and also the clubs. One more big job after this, and I'm done with everything. My sisters up there now. I just want a new start; I don't want to end up dead, you know? Getting shot like a lot of them do 'round here, six feet under with nothing to show for my life." I search my uncle's dark brown, nearly black eyes for any disappointment that might be lurking there, but they have softened with that familiar warmth in his gaze.

The corners of his mouth tip up slightly when he speaks. "Lee, my boy, it would make me such a happy man. I never wanted this life for you or your sister and cousins. This was our choice, mine and your dad's. Things were different back in our day, a lot different. It wasn't about the power trip, it was about respect and not shitting on your own doorstep or robbing someone's Grannie, but you're right—too many lives have been lost along the way." He blows out another plume of smoke. "You better keep in touch with me, boy." I love how he still calls me boy, like I'm four years old, sat on his knee while he cleans his gun with a rag talking to my dad like it's the most natural thing in the world. And maybe it was, for us, anyway. He smiles and wraps his huge arm around my shoulder, dragging me into the house toward the crooning voice of Bob.

We walk into the kitchen where my uncle starts pouring out coffee. Handing me a cup, looking all serious compared to his usual happy-go-lucky self, I can tell the conversation is about to shift. I sit down at the table across from my uncle and look him square in the eyes hoping like fuck this isn't gonna make me want to end this guy even more than I do right now.

"But, son, you're right, Liam needs to disappear one way or another." He lowers his voice and shifts closer to me at the table. Tipping his head, he says; "I heard on the grapevine things about him that would make your toes curl—the wife is close with Liam's Mrs. He has not only beat her bad, but he beat her bad enough he put her in hospital. That boy needs to stop running his mouth about you too." I put down my cup, stand, and thank my uncle for the coffee and catch up. He reaches out and grabs my arm.

"He was at a barbeque with his wife over the weekend, son, was running his mouth, telling people that we both know he's taking you down a peg or two by fucking up the gun drop. We both know that reflects badly on you and this family. It's pissed a lot of people off. Remember what we used to say? Your dad and me? Thou shalt always protect the family. That will never change." His face softens at the mention of family.

"I'll sort it." My uncle gives me a parting hug, slapping me on the back.

"I don't doubt it for a second," he says, releasing me. I head out, my anger barely contained.

I'm soon back in my car. It's dark outside, and the rain is pouring down, pelting like bullets around me. Like it wants to squeeze every breath from my body with every pounding drop as if Satan himself is going to break through the road in front of my car any second and claim my soul and drag it straight to hell with him. My thoughts are as black as the devil himself.

The windscreen wipers clear away a path giving me a perfect view in front of me, the car lights illuminating the dark, quiet street. Sitting back in my seat, I hit the peddle and take off in the direction of Liam's. It's quiet on the roads all the way there, no traffic to speak of. It's like they sense something foreboding is in the air. The silence is deafening and only heightens my thirst for blood; they'd be right to stay home tonight.

Too many times this fucker has taken the piss and let me down. Too many times he's fucked up jobs and made me look bad. I don't like to look bad. The fucker has been beating up his wife. One thing I hate most in this world next to rapists and pedophiles is a woman beating cunt like him. They should all be put on an island together and blown sky fucking high. I will rip his fucking head off for doing this to his wife, a sweet woman with a big kind heart that raises money for so many charities; she lives her life to help others. How she got in tow with Liam fucking Taylor, I'll never know. She doesn't deserve any of his shit when he's nothing but a fucking grassing little rat; an informer to any fucker that will listen. I can't afford to have a loose cannon in my team. People like him only drag the rest of us down with them.

If that makes me a psychopath, then that's what I am. A killer, ridding the world of scum one by fucking one. OK, I have some kind of heart; I do care about people, some people. I have this need deep inside me to protect those people who can't protect themselves. I can't explain it. My emotions are corrupt. I don't care about ridding the world of scum. I only care about my friends and family and people that are weaker than me. Those that cannot defend themselves against the evil in this world. Well, that I can help with.

I heard a noise coming from my father's bedroom. I knew he had been out cold judging by the overwhelming smell of alcohol. When he got home, he was swaying from one side of the hall to the other trying to get to his bedroom. It was quite funny to watch, but I put him to bed before he could cause himself any real damage. I say put him to bed - it was more like I grabbed on for dear life and aimed his body in the general direction of the bed until he face-planted on top of the covers with his clothes still on. All I did was remove his shoes.

I was asleep, but I suddenly woke up to the sound of my father's bedroom door opening - it always made a creaking sound - then what sounded like my dad falling out of bed, so I threw back my quilt and crept out of bed. I took the gun from the drawer in the hallway as I passed and made my way to his room slowly.

I had a horrible feeling in my gut that something wasn't right as I looked at him sprawled before me, he was still in the same place that I had left him in, face down on top of the covers. The dark figure of a man standing over him in black clothes and a balaclava covering his face caught my attention a split second later, and I froze. Just the whites of the strange man's eyes were visible in the dark room. It looked like he was pointing something at the back of my dad's head, something that looked awfully like a sawed-off shotgun. I was no stranger to weapons; I knew what I was looking at.

I was fifteen years old and shaking so hard I was sure that my bones were rattling yet the guy didn't spot me standing in the doorway straight away. With a flash of instinct, I pointed my gun at his head and pulled the trigger, the click of the trigger pulled his attention toward me, and that's when he finally saw me. Realization flickered across his face as the light slowly turned out inside his eyes, his body descending toward the floor, his blood spraying across my dad's bedroom wall like paint. My dad was awake and watching me with fearful eyes, taking in my trembling hands pointing the gun toward the spot where the guy dressed in black was standing only moments before. Now he was clearly fucking dead and slumped on the floor.
"Son...." My dad spoke quietly and calmly as he moved in front of me, but I couldn't lower the weapon. I hadn't even registered him getting off the bed.

"He was going to kill you, Dad." I wanted to shoot that fucker all over again for trying to kill my dad just to make sure he couldn't try it again. A random stranger in the night had changed my life forever; he ripped what little innocence I had left from me in the blink of an eye. I felt almost empty -like he'd taken a part of me with him. How could I kill him so easily, so effortlessly? But if I hadn't, then my dad would be dead right now.

"Shh it's OK, Lee, let's get you back to bed. I'll fix this mess like it never happened, OK? It never happened." Before I knew where I was, I was moving through the air. My dad held me in his arms tight like a protective lion soothing his cub. Taking the gun from my hand, he took me into the bathroom and removed my clothes, turned the shower on, and pushed me under the spray. Washing away the nightmare that had become my life in a split fucking second.

It seemed like time had stood still, and when I blinked again, I was back in my bedroom. I don't remember how I got there or remember my dad putting me there. Everything was a blur. He held me there on my bed while I shook and cried a river of tears into my father's chest until I fell asleep.

I shake myself, looking around and realize I had zoned right out for a second. Slumped in the front seat of my car, remembering the day I took a man's life, the day the man took mine. In my father's eyes, I'd become the man he'd always wanted me to be….

FOUR

Rose

The house is dark when I eventually get myself home; just the small lamp in the living room illuminates beautiful Katie sleeping on the sofa. I reach my hand down and softly shake her arm to wake her.

"Hey, Katie, I'm sorry I'm a little late. How did you and Annie get on with homework?" I ask.

Rubbing at her eyes, she tells me, "Hey. Yeah, clever little girl you've got there, love. She did better than me. Math's was never my strong point – history, yes, math's, no." She looks so tired but smiles regardless, wrapping her arms around me for a hug. I offer to let her sleep over, but she insists on going home, saying she likes the comfort of her own bed. That I understand all too well.

"Thank you again, sweet." I'm so lucky to have found such a caring young woman who absolutely dotes on my baby girl.

"See you tomorrow, love. Oh, and the house phone kept ringing off the hook, but whenever I got to it, they hung up." She smiles before turning, closing the door behind her.

I'm left alone with a sleeping Annie in the next room and my thoughts. Paperwork, that's the only drawback to this job; I hate the paperwork, but it has to be done. I take it to bed with me hoping I can get most of it done before I go into work tomorrow morning. My nights are usually long as I struggle to keep my demons at bay and a certain sexy man out of my head while I tackle the essentials of the refuge.

I shudder as I endeavor to stop thinking about Lee, Dana's friend from school who she grew up with. Turns out he and Dana lived on the same street as my Auntie Nicole, who I used to spend a lot of my time with during the school holidays as a child. Ever since I met him, I haven't been able to get him out of my mind. He's always there smiling at me in my head, annoying the shit out of me with his dominance. I don't take shit from anyone, but he's so bloody bossy I just want to slap that beautiful smile right off his arrogant face while I climb him like a tree.

I will never forget the day I met Lee for as long as I live. I couldn't talk or form any kind of words to say to him at first. He is so unbelievably good looking; I mean panty melting off of a nun's crotch good looking! I thought I would die on the spot—my face burned as bright as the colour of a tomato. I couldn't breathe as he introduced himself to me right there in the women's refuge. He turned up with Logan and Logan's brother, Declan, to rescue us from Dana's crazy ex-husband, Ian, who had broken in and tried to shoot us, killing two police officers in the process. How we got out of that alive, I will never know.

Flipping over to the next page in my paperwork while I get myself comfortable on my bed lying flat on my tummy, I start writing. I soon stop again as Lee's face fills my mind. I sigh with relief that Annie is tucked up in bed asleep; I can't concentrate on this. Jumping off my bed and pulling my nighty over my head I step into the shower to try to take my mind off Lee. The water pelting down over my skin gives me something else to focus on, but like clockwork he fills my mind.
"You should smile more often, baby, it suits you. If you were mine, that beautiful smile would become a permanent fixture on those sweet lips."

I close my eyes as the memory assaults my mind and brings a smile to my lips. I re-live the last time I saw him in the club he owns in our town—I hadn't known until that night it belonged to him.

I went for a drink after work with Dembie; she was working alongside us part-time with the

women's aid as well as doing her tattoos and artwork during the day, but she was on call every night, available when we needed her. Katie worked as a dentist assistant in the high street, but she was also on call for us at night. Being in a women's refuge together with Dana and me, having gone through a similar relationship in the past, brought us all together in a desperate situation and gave us this unbreakable bond that will stand the test of time. We went to a new club in the middle of town, up-market and swanky compared to what we are used to in our small town. I was in my twenties, closer to being thirty give or take a few years. And here I was still broken, still damaged, and quite emotional, looking over my shoulder every time I left the house, every time I went home, every damn day. I wondered if I would ever feel a sense of peace and safety when I went out or would I always carry that with me.

I walked to the bar to ordered another Jack and Coke when I felt hands on my shoulders. I jumped out of my skin, flinching at the touch. Turning around, I saw Dana smiling. "Sorry, didn't mean to scare you, chick," she said, bending forward toward me and kissing me on the cheek.

"Hey, I didn't mean to jump. I don't know why that scared me, just wasn't expecting it I guess," I told her. I hadn't flinched like that in a long time; I really wasn't expecting her to be there.

"I get it." Dana rubbed my arm gently. She really did get me. The way I thought, the way I saw things, the way I acted. She saw that more than anyone else.

The barman brought me my drink and took everyone else's order. Dana threw her arms around me and whispered in my ear. "Rose, I'm so proud of you, bitch tits. You know that, right? Look how far you've came since we got up here. And for pulling together to help others." I almost burst into tears which I tried not to do those days because I didn't want my boo to see the effect Mike, her dad, had on me. I couldn't let my world fall apart; not then, not ever, for her sake.

The bar was filling up with people piling in from work. We joined Dembie at the table where we sat and chatted, catching up and knocking back more drinks than the whole bar full of people in the space of an hour.

"It's all you too. I couldn't do any of it without you. I love you," I told her. She hugged me tighter.

A bartender came toward our table with a bottle of Jack and cans of Coke on a tray. Placing it in front of us he smiled, tipping his head to us. Knowing we hadn't re-ordered, we turned around to look at whoever had sent it over, scanning the tightly-packed room. Lee, Ryan, and Logan were standing there with goofy grins plastered on their faces. They were all wearing black suits, but Lee had his jacket off. His shirt had a few buttons undone showing off his chest. Did I mention he had a great chest? And shiny black curly hair? And a great smile? He was tall, really tall, with a broad chest and shoulders that looked more than capable of holding the world on them. I was smiling at him; I couldn't help it. I wanted to slap myself for enjoying his body right in front of everyone, but I lifted my glass, tilting it toward him in appreciation for the drink and then knocked it back. As I looked at him again, his eyes met mine. I swear they held the hint of a promise, and as his smile grew wider—a smile I knew that was just for me—I rubbed hands along my arms trying to alleviate the chill of the goose bumps that had sprung up on my entire body.
Shit! Double shit!
My heartbeat accelerated. Christ, I wanted to eat him alive, I wanted to feel something more than just fear and panic, and I knew that Lee Young would most likely have me feeling anything but. I was so surprised by the feelings I broke eye contact with him. I didn't want to feel anything. Feelings just hurt you; there's no doubt about it. I knew that first-hand, and it was a painful lesson

I'd learned the hard way. But my body was reacting whether I liked it or not. I lifted my head to see his liquid brown eyes still locked on mine. I poured another drink—he just smiled slightly with his soft full lips. What the hell is he smiling about? I thought my heart was going to stop beating. Its rhythm picked up its pace in my chest, and I was afraid it was going to beat a path right to his feet at any moment.

"Wow, that guy with your man is nice looking. I know I would." Dembie waved her hand at Dana and nudged me in the arm with hers.

"Hey, that's Lee! My old friend from school." Dana giggled.

I turned away and dropped my head toward my drink. The stirrings of desire deep down in my soul overwhelmed me. I knew I had to stay well clear of him. I knew he was a mysterious, dangerous man, and I could never fully trust a man like him. Even if he were an old friend of Dana's, I could never trust another man again.

And then it happened, he was right there crouched down beside me in my chair. I turned to look at him; his eyes were dancing. God, he was so beautiful. I just wanted to touch him, to see that he was real.

"You should smile more often, baby. It suits you. If you belonged to me, that beautiful smile would become a permanent fixture on those sweet lips."

I instantly burst out laughing. "That is the worst pick-up line I have ever heard," I told him. He leaned in farther, his lips inches from my ear, his scent surrounding me. I melted a little more in my chair.
"Maybe…. but it's true. That pretty mouth you got there, your smile would definitely be a permanent fixture while my mouth is attached to the lips of that sweet pussy of yours," he whispered. The rest of the world faded away, and all I could see was him. I closed my eyes as he ran the soft pad of his thumb along my bottom lip while his breath tickled at my ear….

Lee groans gently as I hear the shrill of his phone over his soft breaths, pulling away he stands and walks across the room, pushing through the bar door to make his way outside, needing to take the call. I get up to follow, but I'm stopped by a very drunk man sporting a wet beard. I'm guessing that's where his drink has ended up recently. Grabbing me roughly around the waist, I swayed in his arms from side to side, trying to evade the man's pungent breath as he tried to lean into me.
"Get off me!" I shout.
"Oh come and have a dance with me, love," He slurs, the alcohol clearly making him brave. "I said no, get off me!"

Just as I said the last word, I feel the man's arms leave my waist, being ripped away from me and I watch in horror as he's being dragged outside. I gather my bearings quickly and follow, stumbling out the door in time to see Lee punching the man in the face. I stand in shock waiting for him to notice me there before whirling on my feet and head back indoors with Lee hot on my heels.

Catching up to me, Lee pulled me into the back of the bar. "What the actual fuck. Who was that guy?" I flinched at his aggressive manner; a natural instinct beat into me.

"Just some stupid guy who didn't want to take no for an answer, he's just drunk. You didn't need to hit him." My voice, even to me, sounded mouse-like which made me roll my eyes. Could I be any more pathetic sounding?

Lee's hands wrapped around and twisted in the back of my loose hair tightly. His lips whispered across my ear, "He won't do that again, baby." I had no doubt after the punch he just got.

"I'm calling a taxi, I'm going home," I said. I was panting - Lee's lips were an inch away from mine. I needed to get out of there.

"Hey, Tracey, call a taxi for my girl, Rose, will ya, love?" Lee asked the barmaid while his eyes remained locked on mine. He hadn't moved an inch. He was dressed all in black right down to the gloves. He smelled amazing mixed with the fresh air, but he looked like a serial killer. The thought made me giggle. I felt the fire in my veins for the first time in forever and being that close to him brought back the old me; the woman I used to be—the flirty happy confident me. I liked it. I really liked it. He put me at ease. As quickly as I had felt myself flinch like he sensed it in me, I wanted to wrap my arms around his tall, built frame and beg him to fuck me. God, what had gotten into me? Closing my eyes, I smiled as I felt the sensation flow through my body, feeling turned on for the second time that night. I squeezed my thighs together. The passion rolling off of Lee was intoxicating, and then just as quickly I was snapped out of it.*

"Rose, your taxi's out front." Opening my eyes, he was grinning down at me. He tipped his head, and his lips gently brushed against mine. *"Sleep well, baby,"* he said.

"I will," I said, forcing my legs to move. I made my way outside to the taxi and jumped in. After letting the driver know where to take me, I sat in the back seat still turned on and aching for Lee. But for the first time in a very long time, I knew I was going to sleep well, and that was good.*

Surviving You

The water from the shower sprays so hard over my skin I am sure it takes a layer off. I'm panting, Jesus - I am so turned on remembering how close he was to me. It annoys me that he can get this reaction. Turning off the shower, I dry off and make my way to the bed daydreaming of him, his dark chocolate eyes dancing full of mischief, and that stunning smile plastered on his beautiful face. All of it - just for me. Pulling the covers over my head, I fall into a deep sleep with the light still on and dreaming of Lee.

Chapter Five

Lee

My windscreen wipers move back and forth, clearing away the rain that continues to fall as I pull up a few blocks away from Liam's flat. Parking the car, I pull my thoughts from my teenage self and into the man I am now, focusing on what is ahead. Once I turn the ignition off I'm surrounded by darkness and deathly silence. The only lights on in the street are the dimly-lit street lamps and the few lights left on in people's homes. Pulling my gun from my inside pocket I shove it into the top of my jeans, double checking my knife is still in its sheath at my hip. Pulling the black balaclava over my head, I slip my gloves over my hands. I move quietly and slowly out of the car, dipping my body down by the side so I'm out of sight. I push the door shut and wince when it clicks louder than I had intended it to. Leaning against my car, I wait for the longest of moments to make sure the coast is clear. The only sound I can hear is my ragged breathing. I watch the condensation coming out of my mouth like puffs of smoke in front of my face, willing my heart to steady. It's cold and wet out here, but my adrenaline is pumping through my veins.

Running into one of the gardens in front of me, I throw my body over the wooden fence ducking down again once I land. Crawling underneath and along the bottom of what I assume to be a living room window, I make my way to the next wooden fence and clear it same as the first one. I feel like fucking Spider-Man on crack except I don't have special fucking powers. I make it to Liam's garden and thank fuck he's let the grass grow to knee height—the lazy bastard. I crawl my way through until I hit the wall at the side of his bottom floor flat. I stand in the dark and slide my body along the wall.

"Bit late for a social visit, mate," a strong Irish accent whispers at my side. Turning my head toward the voice while my heart beats out of my chest, I clap eyes on a welcome sight—the fucking dick scared me to death. I would recognize that voice anywhere. My gaze lands on Ryan, and I smile into the pitch black as I pat him on the shoulder.

"Yeah, it is. What the fuck are you doing? I told you I got this."

Ryan, raising his hand toward his face holding the torch under his chin and grinning like a Cheshire fucking cat, he proceeds to inform me, "I wasn't letting you have all the fun now, was I, mate? I miss out on so much as it is." The torch lights up his whole face as he growls into it. His sparkling, mischievous, light-brown eyes go cross-eyed, his jet black hair and beard making him look pure fucking evil. If I didn't know the crazy bastard so well even, I would be scared of him. He is a professional boxer, shorter than me at around five eight, slim build but as strong as an ox, fast on his feet and ripped to perfection. The ladies fucking love him. I've seen him put a six-foot-four- inch man who was built like a tank on his ass with one punch. Knocked him clean out. Like I said – crazy bastard.

Making my way to the back of the house where the back door is, the rain continues to beat down on me, soaking me to the bone. I shiver slightly—part cold, part anticipation. Removing the knife from my hip sheath and sliding it along the door seam, it pops right open for me, and a smile spreads across my face at how fucking easy it is. I slide my body inside the dank kitchen; I know the layout like the back of my hand as I've been in here enough times before. Ryan makes his way into another room taking a look around. This man always has my back even when I don't fucking want or need it— it's very much appreciated.

Before I know it, I'm in Liam's bedroom. He's lying in bed, out for the count which surprises me 'because the fucker is always wide-eyed and bushy-tailed, suffocating his body with coke and Christ

knows what else. I'm standing in the shadows watching and waiting, listening to the sound of his shallow breathing, making sure there's no one else in here with him. My hand is itching to pull out my gun and fill him with bullets, but I put a lid on that thought for the moment. I need him to be aware of what's happening. I need him to look into my eyes when the lights go out. Liam suddenly jolts awake, and I know he can see my shadow in the dark at the end of his bed. Fuck... I launch myself forward lifting my fist up into the air, my knuckles connecting with his nose making it crack beneath my fist. The feeling is mildly liberating. He tries to land a punch back at my face, but I move too fast for him, and he misses me, his body following his fist as he falls haphazardly on the floor with a loud thud. I can hear his breathing quicken as fear grips him and he tries to figure out who's paying him a visit in the small hours of this wet morning. He's scared out of what's left of his Goddamn, fucked up mind. Good, he should be. My smile lights up my face under the balaclava that covers it; the adrenaline coursing through my body gives me that rush I know oh so well. I don't want it but it's there, and I'll embrace it all the same.

"Who the hell are you?" he shouts wildly, a dramatic plea begging to know who is attacking him. Little does he know I am there to take his pathetic little life away from him and free his wife and the world of his poison. His eyes bore into me from where he sits on the floor. Bringing his knees up in front of him, he pushes his body away from me slowly, his chest rising and falling as the panic starts to set in. I can see the fear flash clearly in his eyes—I can smell it, and he reeks of it which only feeds my thirst to break his neck.

"Who the fuck are you?" he shouts out into the dark again. I don't answer but instead pull my gun from my jeans. He's on me before I can take aim at his filthy fucking face. As we are sparring, Ryan makes his way inside the room behind me. Managing to get control of myself, I aim my gun at Liam's legs and blow his kneecaps off for him. He screams like a fucking banshee before he rolls about on the floor holding onto himself, the pain written all over his face. He's not down for long, though, and in seconds he flies at me with all of the strength he has left in him. The crazy fucker is trying to pull my balaclava free from my face, the stupid cunt. I wrap my arm around his neck to stop him from moving; rage is burning through my veins. I don't even flinch when he tries to remove himself from my hold—the thirst inside me to squeeze his windpipe and remove the very breath and life from his soulless body vibrates through my bones. Nothing ever felt so good than to seek retribution for the abuse he gave to others. It's what all these fuckers deserve. Nothing less. The darkness takes control of me and won't let go. I lift the gun to his head, forcing it into his temple. My eyes lock with Ryan's, but he doesn't need to say anything. We silently communicate with each other with our eyes to convey all that needs to be said with a subtle movement of the head. Get this done and dusted, get the mess cleaned up, and get the fuck out. Simple, really.

I pull the trigger and put a bullet into Liam's brain and watch as his head flies sideways. Bits of flesh, blood, bone, and brain matter splatters across the walls. I feel the life drain away from his body; it turns limp and lifeless as he falls to the cold floor. His life turns to nothing to dust like he was never here, disappearing straight to hell where the fucker belongs. I drag his body across the room using all of the strength I can muster to pull him. The strong stench of his sweat pours from his body, mingling with the copper tang of blood, assaulting my nose as I move him. Dropping him when I reach the bed, Ryan and I move the fuck out of there before his wife comes home to this shit storm. How will she react? Who knows? Here's hoping she sees her freedom painted on the wall with her husband's brain.

My phone buzzes in my pocket ten minutes from home, "What's up, mate?" I pause, listening to a frantic voice. "What the fuck? Be there in ten." It was Logan, something about a fire. He was talking

so fast I couldn't understand his thick Scottish accent. Fuck - I hope nobody I know has been hurt. My thoughts instantly snap to Rose. I hope she's not hurt or her little girl. Something tightens in my chest, strangling my heart. I put my foot down and beg the higher powers that everyone is safe.

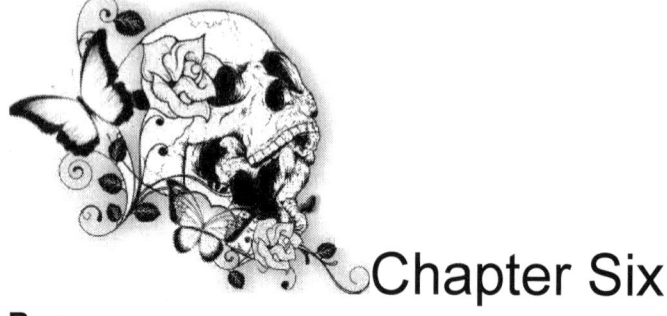

Chapter Six

Rose

At the back of six o'clock in the morning, most mornings, there he is. The predator. A hot as all hell, male, stallion-like creature that moves with such speed as he runs by. He has my full attention every single time he runs past my front garden, along my street, and then along the back of my house, turning down the next street and then onto Park Hill. In nothing but shorts and a tee in all kinds of weather; he still manages to run and look good doing it. It's bitter cold out there this morning, yet there he is, running by my house looking all beautiful, hot, and perfect. He has every hair on my body standing up on end.

Sipping back my first caffeine fix of the morning, I watch him jog by. My eyes rake him in from head to toe. His t-shirt hugs his torso like it was made just for him; I can just see the lines of his eight pack through the fabric soaked with sweat, his muscles bulging at the sleeves. And there's something about his shorts—the way they cling to his ass, his junk bulging in front— that does all kinds of weird flighty shit to my body. I ignore the tingling belly flutters while clenching my thighs together to try and stop the ache between my legs as I sip back more hot coffee. I watch him move farther away from me in a daze and sigh as he leaves my sight.

"Oh, my. That ass in those shorts. Those dark chocolate dancing eyes. Christ, his body is to die for," I whisper into my coffee I'm sipping, I try and pull myself together again, the desire stirring in my core burning me up deep inside. I would love to sit on his face; his talented tongue on my pussy any day of the week would probably feel like heaven. If I was just a bit braver... I bet he's a professional pussy muncher. I giggle to myself at the thought. But I cannot go there, I chastise myself. I don't even like him, I think he's an arrogant know-it-all pig, and he scares the shit out of me. That dangerous, almost mysterious, manner he has about him. Bloody hell, I think I actually love him. Is it even possible to love and hate someone at the same time? He's everywhere - in my dreams replacing the hideously terrifying dark nightmares that have me up all night. He haunts them in such a delicious way—his beauty and passion for life crept in chasing off the demons in my head. He's all I see when I close my eyes in the dark, all I see when I wake up at dawn. But he's an arrogant, angry shit in real life. Even so it appears all that is Lee, his beautiful dark eyes burning into my very soul, his soft full lips - oh what I would do to feel them on mine. The feel of his hands on my body, his solid frame against mine in my bed. His stunning, all-genuine smile makes me beam without knowing I'm doing it. I am so glad he's there in my head, in my dreams filling them up, the only place I can have him, the only place I can touch and be with him. The safest place I'll ever be while locked in his warm embrace. It's burned into my brain and my very existence.

I will not let myself get caught up with a hot guy or any hot guy for that matter, not ever again, not after what Mike did to me. I can never trust another man again. I can look, and I can wonder what it would feel like to have his mouth on mine and on my body, but that is all.

I give my head a wobble, finish my coffee, and get ready to drop Annie, my boo, off at school and myself to work. Watching him had me daydreaming of possibilities the ideas in my head over… for now.

Manchester is my home, and I love it! You can take the girl out of Manchester, but you can't take Manchester out of the girl. Mad-chista, as it's known by many Manc's alike. Anyone that has lived here or has travelled to go clubbing or for a night out knows the nightlife is one of the best. A close second to London. I've been to a lot of gigs and had some of the best nights out in the city center. Believe me, it gets very messy. I met Mike at a gig, and I fell hook, line, and sinker as soon as I set eyes on him. He was sitting behind the rest of the band on stage playing the drums; that boy can play, he was mesmerizing to watch. He saw me watching him throughout the song, locking his gaze on me like he was playing just for me, and then after they stopped playing he disappeared backstage. A short while later he came looking for me. I was sitting at the bar drinking back my Jack when I should have just gone home. Hindsight is such a beautiful thing. Little did I know that it was all tits up from there. I wish I could go back to that night and get the fuck out of there. Had I known then what I know now, I would have been out of there like a freaking shot and ran for the hills.

You couldn't have met a nicer person than Mike when I first met him; I guess it was all part of the illusion. Not long into our relationship he started taking drugs and drinking everything he could get his hands on and inevitably my life turned into one long dark nightmare, going turning downhill real fast. Every night he turned into a complete stranger—a monster. I hated him with a passion. I realized I had to get the hell out of there as soon as I could, and that's exactly what I did. I didn't want him turning on our daughter Annie the way he turned on me.

I cannot believe how different our lives are now that I have my own cafe with my best friend, Dana. And I get to work every day with some truly awesome friends and people. My daughter, Annie Boo, is finally happy and settled in a new school with new friends; she's the happiest I have ever seen her.

Dana is the happiest I have ever seen her too; moving to Scotland was the best thing that could have happened to all of us. Dana and Logan have just had a beautiful baby boy, Jayden. He weighed a healthy 7lb 2 oz. when he came kicking and screaming into the world. He's the spitting image of his Dad.

Lee is away a lot working and visiting his family in Manchester but when he's home I feel a lot safer in my own skin. He's kind of got that gangster cheeky happy go lucky thing about him; he could charm his way out of a prison cell. Who knows – maybe he did. I know he served time, but it wasn't long.

SEVEN

Dana

I saw someone running with a bottle in their hand. A man, definitely a man. The bottle was on fire as I watched him run, wondering how he hadn't set his clothes on fire yet or burnt his skin. I watched the flames swing back and forth, his powering arms pushing him forward alongside his legs and it came to me like a slow, single light bulb in my brain waking me up. It's a fire bomb, and it's heading my way.

"Fuck." The second my eyes catch up with my brain, smoke fills the air all around me. "Jesus." I can't move. "Oh my God."

The flames rip through my house so fast I can barely think; my body and my mind push my legs through the blaze by instinct toward the stairs. I run up to my babies' bedroom, adrenaline pumping through my body as I hit the top of the stairs and frantically shout out my babies' names, choking on the thick fog of smoke. Thankfully, Kayleigh and Amy are in Jayden's room pulling Jayden out of his cot, screaming and coughing. It got so dark so fast we can't see a damn thing; the smoke is getting so thick everywhere I look turns black.

"Shit." I pull my babies into my side and throw a robe around them in a feeble attempt at trying to shield them from the blaze. "We have to move - let's go," I say into the thick, dark, smoke-filled room, moving my babies toward the door. The heat is getting so intense and frightening I'm sure we won't make it out. I move faster into the hallway, ushering the children along and down the stairs. Kayleigh and Amy scream as part of the roof falls on the top of the stairs behind us, crashing and crackling above our heads. Something hits me in the face, but I keep moving; there is no time to stop. I manage to reach the front door and push us through, out into the dark street, falling onto the pavement as we struggle to suck in the air. I wrap my arms around my three children, crying in utter relief. I catch sight of Declan sprinting toward us.

"Dana, are you all OK? Logan?" he shouts with a terrified look in his eyes.

"He's not here; he's overworking in the club office." He kneels down and wraps his arm tight around us.

"Thank fuck you're all OK." I look up to see Lee running toward us, and when I looked up at him, I can see in his eyes that he thought the same thing that Declan had just a few minutes ago. I reach out to him and grab his forearm, but he is already wrapping me up in his arms.

With a look of dread, I tell him, "Logan's not here." With that, the sirens fill the air echoing all around us and ringing in our ears. Fire engines, ambulances, and the police roar along the street, vehicles screeching to a halt as they all pile out and spring into action.

"Katie!" I screech into the dark burning street lit up by the orange and yellow flames. I look to my friend's house a few doors down and see the raging flames whirling out through the windows of her house.

"Katie!" I scream out again. Scrambling up, I start running toward the house but don't get very far. Just before I reach her house, an arm wraps its way around my waist pulling me back forcefully. "Declan, let me go!" I scream, begging him harder when windows explode sending shattered glass flying through the air toward us.

"Katie!" I scream at her house, willing her to walk out through her flame-filled front door. Rose is at my side within seconds with Annie in her arms and Lee's huge arms wrapped tightly around her waist holding her back the same way Declan is holding me. She's screaming in pain right here beside me.

"She has to come out. Please come out," Rose whispers into Annie's hair.

I look into her big brown eyes and whisper back, "She has to. She just has to."

I turn back, eyes on the blazing building, but I don't know what to do. I hear Declan at my back talking into his phone, his words incomprehensible. It's like he isn't really here and this isn't really happening.

The firemen move us back to the other side of the road and get to work. Rose and I plead with them to find Katie and get her the hell out of the quickly burning house. Declan keeps a tight hold on me while the firemen unravel hoses and begin dousing the fire. A few disappear through the front door while two more climb a ladder up to Katie's bedroom window. Water is flying into the blaze, thick black smoke whirls up into the air, and all I can do is stand there with my friends. Helpless. With my heart in my mouth, breathing hard, I watch the firemen try to do their job. The longer it takes, the more I know deep down that I won't see my best friend ever again.

EIGHT

Rose

I stare into the blackness; the fire is nowhere to be seen, and the street is dark again. The only light I can see comes from the street lamps. I'm glad a strong arm is holding me up as I can barely keep my legs from buckling under me. I need that strength.

"You're OK. You're safe, baby," Lee whispers into my hair, holding me against his solid warm body. It is only then I realize I am shivering. I turn my gaze toward where Dana and now Logan are standing, and the kids who stand there in a huddle. Lee, Waff, Vicky, and Mandy are by our sides too. Katie is gone; she didn't stand a chance, and now she's dead. Gone - just like that. She had been sleeping; she wasn't aware of what was happening around her, the smoke she had inhaled filled up her lungs and killed her then the blaze took over until there was nothing left of her or her house. It's like she never existed.

My heart aches like I have been stabbed in the chest repeatedly; a vice squeezes it so tight that it's almost difficult to breathe. Three homes are burned— completely burned to the ground and one life gone. Logan, Lee, Ryan, and Declan look into each other's eyes communicating to each other with just one look—a silent conversation between them—to move us out of there to a safer place and that's what they do. Ushering us away from the carnage surrounding us.

I throw back the brandy Lee had handed to me and immediately hand the empty glass right back to him. I need another one or four. The whole bottle would do, but I doubt it would numb the ache in my heart—the pain is too much to bear. He hands me another full glass and sets the bottle on the coffee table in front of me before throwing back his own glass.

"Better?" he asks with warmth and concern in his deep tone.

"Better, thank you. And thanks for putting us up here for the night in your home."

He leans forward and strokes my jaw with his thumb while holding my cheek in his hand, searching my face with his dark eyes locking on mine. They bore into me while he remains silent. My body reacts in so many different ways. My nipples stand to attention, and I swallow as I close my eyes. My core tightens, a reaction to the sensation from the warm, soft touch to my face. His fingers stroking my skin awaken the arousal all over my body. My thighs clench tighter together.

Opening my eyes, I notice he is wearing dark jeans and a black tee—he looks so delicious. His dark brown hair is almost black, a mass of messy tight curls that I want to run my hands through then down his tee to feel his chest and toned abs. I push his hand away from my face feeling almost embarrassed at the way my body reacts to his touch and reach for the brandy bottle. Pouring myself another drink, I try to push away all I was feeling for him deep down into my stomach, denying myself to feel it. I want him. I really want him. This is so messed up, I think to myself as I throw back my drink and place the glass back down on the coffee table.

Lee has moved closer to me; I can feel the heat from his body before I even see him. He tucks a lock of my hair slowly behind my ear, his fingers brushing over the skin there as he moves his hand along the nape of my neck and places his other hand on my hip. I can't move or breathe. The sensation of his touch feels like electric bolts shooting through my whole body, heating me up, moving through me from my head right down to my toes. I feel myself closing my eyes overcome by desire and need. I am so turned on but full of fury for having these feelings while my friend is dead. He is so close to me his scent encircles me, wrapping me up, and I swear it has me crumbling further. His lips crash down on mine, his tongue swiping across my lips delicately at first before I feel the nip of his teeth on my bottom lip. I'm sure my legs are going to melt from under me. His lips are so soft and warm, his tongue slides into my mouth and duels with mine, sending my insides to mush. Mind-blowing tingles feather my skin as I melt into his arms. His hands run through my long, dark waves, stroking gently. It belies what is to come next as I am thrust into the wall. His huge toned body pins me there as he tips his face inches away from mine. I can smell the brandy on his breath. I can smell the scent of him, and it sends me wild. Moving my lips along to his neck, I press soft kisses around his throat. He grinds his hard cock into my belly, and I suck in a sharp breath, conscious of my arousal soaking my knickers. I'm overwhelmed and confused; I don't know if I can do this with him, no matter how much my body needs it.

"I don't know if I can, Lee," I sigh, regret in my voice." Isn't it wrong after what's happened?" Whispering into his lips, tears streak from my eyes, rolling down my cheeks into both of our mouths. Backing me up again, he reaches his other arm above my head where his other hand has my own hands pinned against the wall, stroking his fingers gently – oh-so-gently down my arm and over the side of my breast. I moan at the contact, thoughts of anything else disappearing, the intensity in his eyes so full of lust, want, and need. Closing my eyes, I savour the feeling, his soft lips lapping away at my tears.

"I know you want me, Rose, just as much I want you. I'll make you feel so good, baby, come so hard. I need to taste that sweet pussy." He's almost begging, and I can hear the desire he has for me in every syllable.

What the hell...My mind is telling me a different story than my body; they are at war with each other. I give in, slumping against the wall. His eyes sweep over my body as he pulls off my cami top to reveal my black, lace bra. His teeth sink into my bottom lip, the pain sending an electric jolt straight down into my now-soaked knickers. I've never been this turned on—hungry for more—in my entire life. I tremble and shiver against his dominant body, his words vibrating through me. Jesus, I feel like I am lost. I can't think straight.

"I will make love to you, fuck you hard until you're begging me for release. Until your legs tremble. Until your pussy aches with need, thirsty for more. Is that what you want?" He punctuates his words with harsh kisses in-between." I want you to come long and hard for me, baby." He slides a strong hand down toward the hem of my skirt then hitches it slowly upwards until my legs are naked before him, and my knickers are exposed to him. Strong fingers hook into the side of the fabric, and with a sharp tug he rips them away from my body. He grins at me, lifting the scrap of fabric in front of my face. With a twinkle in his eye, he leans forward and rubs his nose along the wet fabric. "Mmm," he moans as he closes his eyes. Wow!

"Lee, will you just touch me?" I snap angrily, more at myself for feeling this way about the incredibly arrogant, beautiful man standing in front of me smelling my knickers. Without a word, his grip on my wrists above my head tightens, and he snaps off the clasp at the front of my bra with his teeth. His lips clamp around my swelling nipple while his other hand works between my thighs, pushing them open. His intense dark eyes catch mine for a split second. He looks pained. My eyes close as the pleasure takes over and his finger slides inside my folds upwards inside of me, my walls stretching with his strong fingers.

"Oh yes, Lee, yes," is all I can manage. I moan loudly as his thumb works my clit. His fingers dive in deeper. It's so wantonly delicious.

"Look at me, Rose," he growls. "Look at me." My body is vibrating with need as I watch his blazing eyes cutting into me, his own pleasure building as he drives me higher and higher. In the background, Lee's phone starts ringing and vibrating on the kitchen counter, but he ignores it and

keeps working me. Both of us are lost in the moment.
"Lee!" I scream out, a loud, "Oh my God" following as I explode around his fingers. He removes both hands from me, and I slide down the wall trying to catch my breath. I'm panting so goddamned hard. Lee takes my hands and pulls me up into his arms, moving me to his sofa where I slump into the cushions like a wet noodle. He hands me my bra and top which I scramble to put on, feeling utterly vulnerable, and I don't like it. The noise coming from his phone brings me back like a smack in the face to reality, so I place my hands on his shoulders and push him away, breathing hard. His chest is rising and falling so fast.
The intense lust in his eyes burns into me while he whispers into my hair, "You're quite something else, shorty." Shaking his head, he moves away and turns, walking into the kitchen to answer the call.

Grabbing the bottle of brandy from the coffee table, I knock it back while I sit there watching him. My glare burns holes in the back of his head, trying to steady my breathing. What in the hell just happened? I hear him speaking, but I can't really make out what he is saying or who he is talking to. I fill my glass that I abandoned earlier on the coffee table and throw the burning liquid down my throat. As I sit there on Lee's huge sofa trying to compose myself and failing miserably, I quickly burst into tears, burying my face in the cushion. The tears flow as I sob for one of my best friends. They flow for whatever the hell just happened with Lee. It can't happen again. I drift off into an uneasy sleep, exhausted from the day from hell.

I vaguely remember being woken by the feel of strong arms and a solid body at my back holding me tight to him, whispering in my ear.

"I've got you, baby. I've got you." He holds me, stroking my hair for what seems like hours in an attempt to shield me from my own pain.

NINE

Lee

I take the call from Logan. I knew he would be checking in on Rose; both he and Dana would be worried about her state of mind after losing her home and one of her girls in the same night. It's a fucking heart-breaking situation.

Rose is crying again. I look in on her quietly; she looks so fucking good in my bed. She had fallen asleep earlier on my sofa, so I eventually carried her into my bedroom and placed her on my bed, covering her, making her comfortable and then I watched her sleep for a while. Under no circumstances am I leaving her side. This little waif of a woman brings out that protective side of me, and I can't help but indulge the urge. She's the most beautiful woman I've ever seen in my life; I can't help but think she's now even more broken because of me. With each sob I hear tearing from her throat, my heart bleeds like it's being ripped out of my chest and stamped on by God himself. My soul is being sent further and further into the abyss, and I want to take away all of her pain and hold it in my heart so that she can be free of it. Free of the torture, free of the guilt that consumes her.

Surviving You

This is my fault. I should not have let all of this happen in the first place, but I was too busy trying to wrap things up back home to check on security. I've slipped up well and truly. I'm such a fuck up
—I couldn't protect them; my friends, all of them could have died. And Rose, if she had been taken away from me tonight I might as well have put a bullet in my brain here and now. She doesn't realize it yet, but she's mine, she always will be. No matter how selfish it is, I just can't walk away. I know she feels what I feel deep inside her heart, past all of the mist that clouds her judgment. Past all of the hurt that she's endured before. I need her to take a chance on me, need her to believe I would never hurt her. Every time I think about her, every time I see that stunning face looking back at me, every time my eyes fall on her… she instantly makes my cock. Such a beautiful and beguiling creature.

I open my bedroom door, and my heart aches for her. My blood is boiling in my veins thinking of earlier. When I find these fuckers, I'm going to rip them apart with my bare fucking hands.

"Baby, please don't cry," I say as I sit down on the edge of the bed next to her. Sweeping her hair out of her beautiful eyes, I see the sorrow and pain ripping her apart inside. Sweeping my thumbs across her cheeks, I wipe the tears from under her eyes. "I'm so sorry for everything that has happened. I can't bring Katie back, I can't undo any of this, but I'm going to fix what I can." I gulp down my anger, keeping my voice soft so as not to frighten her. "I swear I know that isn't enough... I should have been here." The guilt rips me up inside as I watch her body vibrate with her sobbing and her own guilt.

"It's not your fault, Lee, none of this is your fault. We didn't see it coming, either; we let our guard down, and this is the result of our stupidity. If anything it's my fault. We should never have done that

—we got too comfortable as the time passed. I thought we were free from all of this. I thought I was finally free." Her voice breaks on the last word, her head hitting my chest as her fingers fist in my tee and her tears soak me. I take it all from her, giving her the comfort she needs until she can't cry another tear and she falls asleep exhausted from the pain. I lay her back down on the bed wrapping her up in my arms, and I hold on tight, never wanting to let her go. It is so comfortable and natural, soon my eyes slip closed as I drift off right alongside my love.

The light is shining brightly through the window when I wake. Rose is still in the same position she fell asleep in. Moving slowly so as to try not to move her, I reach out and stroke her long dark hair out of her face. I nuzzle into her neck breathing in her scent that drives me insane and whisper in her ear, "Are you awake, beautiful?" Her breathing changes from a slow pace picking up speed, and I know she's with me, feeling everything I'm feeling. My cock is growing inside my boxers with just the feel of her soft, warm body against mine and having her here in my bed. I never bring any woman back here, ever; I never want her to leave.

She turns her head and smiles. "Hey, I'm sorry I fell asleep I..." she stammers.

"Shh, you needed it. Besides, I like you being here with me." She stares up at me with a quizzical look in her dark brown eyes. I take her face into my hands, tilting her head up and brushing my thumb across her soft lips, placing my lips over hers in a soft, gentle kiss. I don't want my movements to push her away from me or to scare her off completely when she's so fragile, so I move as slowly as possible, my body fighting the urge to take her and fuck her hard into the mattress. Her moan against my lips tells me she wants this, but her eyes tell a different story. I can see her mind is fighting against what her body is telling me it wants. Her eyes slowly close as the kiss deepens, and she instantly melts into my body as I pull her in closer. My tongue slips into her mouth and finds hers dueling together as one. It's like she's been made just for me. Every hair on my body stands up as my body ignites. My fingers twist in her hair, her hands wrap around my neck, and my body shakes as she tugs at my hair. Her hands trail down the back of my neck and travel the length of my back. A strangled groan escapes into her mouth as I struggle to keep my composure. Digging her nails into my skin, her breathing speeds up as my hand smothers her breast, and I knead it, rolling her swollen nipple through the thin material of her tank top.

Surviving You

I break out of the kiss and drag her top up over her head revealing her black, lace bra. I lose it completely. I unclip her bra and throw it across the room not caring where it lands. She's magnificent; perfect breasts with hard pink nipples begging for my touch—begging to be adored. My mouth and hands beg to adore them. The air is thick with our arousal. My cock is rock fucking hard, and my mind is screaming at me to fuck her fast and hard, but I know I'm going too fast for her and risking everything. I don't want to lose her before I've really got her. All of he— mind, body and soul.

She moans into my mouth and nips at my bottom lip with her teeth. Fuck! I want to lose myself in her and her in me. I can feel the arousal pouring off her in waves; she's hungry, fuck - I'm hungry for her. Fuck it, I can't hold on much longer, I need to be balls deep inside her and make her scream my name. I want to hear my name from those lips of hers. I gaze into her eyes asking for permission, what I see reflected back tells me all I need to know. I unzip the side of her skirt and peel it from her hips, dragging it down her gorgeous legs. I forgot that I'd brutally ripped her underwear from her earlier so I am gloriously surprised when she finally lays before me absolutely naked. And boy, is that a fucking sight to behold.

She never takes her eyes off me, watching my every move as I slide down her body, nipping and kissing as I go. I spread her legs apart lapping at her folds with my tongue. I love that she's already soaking wet. Trailing my tongue over her clit she pushes her hips into my face, and I can't help the growl that comes from my chest—she tastes so fucking good. I lap and torture her until she's right on the edge ready to explode. Removing my mouth, I hover over, grasping her hips tightly. She's killing me, absolutely killing me. As I run my hands up and down her breasts and stomach, my gaze never leaving hers, my hard cock prods at her entrance. Closing my eyes, I push deep inside her and feel all my dreams coming true in one thrust. She's so tight she feels like nothing I've ever felt before. I try desperately hard to keep control of myself—this woman laid bare before me has the power to undo me in seconds. I don't want to embarrass myself by coming too soon, but fuck...I squeeze my eyes tight and take a deep breath.

"Lee." Shit. Panicking that she's changed her mind, I see her eyes are wide and full of guilt. I pull my cock from her sweet, tight pussy cursing under my breath. She stares up at me with a confused look on her face.

"Baby, it's OK. I know." And I do; I know right then that I pushed too fast. I lower my head in shame, unable to look at her.

"No, Lee. I'm sorry."

"Hey, it's OK. It's too soon. I'm so sorry, baby." She reaches her hand up and cups my face, her eyes soft, her expression shocking the shit out of me. She cranes her neck up, and her lips brush against mine, nipping my bottom lip and continuing to trail kisses along my jaw and down my neck, her fingers languidly stroking their way down my chest and abs. That slither of light shining in her eyes has dared me to hope.

"You're killing me, baby," I whisper in her ear. Her hand strokes down to my cock then she wraps her fingers around me. I push her down and pin her back to the bed, sliding my cock inside her sweet pussy again. I groan into her hair; her nails dig into my back as I slide in and out of her, feeling her pussy clamp tight around my cock. Thrusting my hips forward, I relish the ecstasy that fills my veins. My breathing is coming thick and fast—my body has ignited for her. Her hips push forward to meet mine. She's so close to letting go, I can feel her velvety walls squeezing my cock. Gripping her hips tight, I thrust harder a few more times before I feel her milking my cock, exploding around me as her orgasm hits. It pushes my release to the forefront, and all I can think about is emptying myself inside her. I rock her hips farther into me, and as her walls clamp on tight, I explode deep inside her, the blood rushing to my head and my roar echoing around the room.

TEN

Rose

I return to my office after running a few last minute errands before going out shopping tonight. Shopping is the last thing I want to do, but Annie and I both need new clothes; we lost everything in the fire. I hear a voice coming from the office. Tossing my handbag on the counter, I head there to see what's going on.

"Rose, is that you?" Dana calls from the other room. "Yes, it's me," I shout.

I move behind the counter to make a skinny vanilla latte and begin sipping at it as Dana rounds the corner. I smile at her as she moves in front of me. She plants a kiss on my cheek; I like that we can share that kind of affection so easily.

"Are you OK, chick?" I ask. "Yeah, I'm surviving. Are you?"

Setting my latte down in front of me, I respond, "I didn't get much sleep last night."

By the look on her face, I can tell she didn't get much shut-eye either. After what happened to our dearest friend, I hadn't wanted to leave the safety of Lee's house. All I want to do is hide away, curl up into a ball, and shut out the world. To put myself out of this misery. I don't know how I am supposed to understand what happened. It all happened so fast, and I'm having trouble dealing with it, I've never experienced anything like it in my life. The pain in my heart just won't disappear.

"It's OK," I faintly hear through my cries. When I lift my head, I see Dana's eyes filled with the same pain that fills mine. She sits beside me at the table and lays her hand on my arm, gently stroking it with trembling thumbs. The side of her face is bruised and slightly swollen from something falling inside her house and hitting her. Luckily, the firemen managed to put the fire out in her house before it caused too much damage. Fortunately, she didn't lose it all.

"Tell me what I can do to help." Her voice is worried, and her eyes are nothing but a display of her pity mixed with her own pain. I can't even think about speaking as my tears soak into my top. She takes my hand in hers, folds her fingers through mine, and holds on tight. Just having her hold my hand makes me cry harder. I'm a blubbering mess.

"I'm sorry this happened," she says, her eyes welling with tears. My hand is clenched around hers, and we hold on tight to one another for a long time.

"One day I promise we will be free of all of this," she grits out. I just nod my head and start to think about how I can kill Mike, a hundred different scenarios racing through my head. How sick does that make me? A broken woman fantasising about how to kill another human being. What has he done to me?

Mustering up the courage to smile, I say, "As much as I want to sit here and pour out my heart, you must excuse me, Dana, while I get myself together and get ready to go get some supplies and, most importantly, clothes." I laugh a little at the irony of starting all over again. I start to feel heat gather in my cheeks as the embarrassment of crying all over my closest friend creeps in. I order a taxi to come and collect me in twenty minutes. I needed to get out of there and stay busy—it is the only thing keeping me remotely sane.

After I get what I need, taking no joy in shopping the way I usually do, I make my way back to Lee's. There is nobody there when I arrive so I dump our stuff on the sofa and start putting away the food I bought. Even though he doesn't need anything, it makes me feel better knowing I am doing something—anything. My phone pings in my bag. Pulling it out and reading the message icon, I see a text message from Lee. It makes me smile.

Lee - *Where are you?*

I quickly reply while putting the milk into the colossal fridge.

Rose - *At your house.*

He responds immediately.

Lee - *Good stay there I want to see you, are you still staying over tonight?*

A small smile creeps over my lips as I reply.

Rose - *Sure if that's OK.*

He replies double quick again.

Lee - *Of course it's OK stay as long as you want.*

My small smile turns into an enormously stupid grin. Hopping off the bar stool, I walk over to the kettle and switch it on. As I'm typing out my next text, the phone begins ringing in my hand, displaying Lee's name and his gorgeous face on the screen.

"Make me a coffee while you're making one."

"What. Where are you? You can see me?" I ask, spinning around the room looking for him.

He lets out a sigh then questions, "You going to make me one or not?" I pull out another cup from the cupboard and start making two cups of coffee.

"Where are you, Lee?" I can hear the smile on his face as his voice turns husky.

"I'm right here." And he is. He comes right through the front door looking all kinds of sexy, the huskiness in his voice snaking its way through my body and awakening every nerve ending. I shiver as he makes his way toward me. I turn and pick up his coffee and hand it to him. I'm nervous. Not scared, but definitely nervous. I'm well aware of who Lee really is and what circles he travels in and just how dangerous he is. I slept in his bed last night, and then I went on and let my body give into the magnetic pull he has on me. I question my sanity continuously.

"I can see that," I say, laughing at how easy this seems for him.

He smiles down at me, his chocolate eyes sparkling mischievously, sending shivers through my body. My thighs clench together under his intense stare. Placing my coffee down, I move to walk around him, but his enormous arm snakes around my waist stopping me from going anywhere. He puts his cup down next to mine and wraps me in his arms. Slipping my hands around his waist under his tee, I curl into him, savoring his comfort.

"I like this too much," I breathe. "Being here with you."

"I like you being here with me too," he says, moving back to look into my eyes. "I meant what I said; you can stay here as long you need."

"I know, thank you. I appreciate that, I do, but I have to get something sorted out for Annie. I need her to have some routine and for her to feel settled even though we lost our home. I..." He stops me from saying anything else, placing his finger over my lips gently.

"I want to keep you safe, baby. Both of you. Let me keep you safe."

I run my fingers down the front of his tee as I tell him, "I want you, Lee, you know I do. I want to be with you, but you have to show me the real you."

"Be careful what you wish for, Rose," he tells me, a cheeky grin crossing his face.

"I think we had a very lucky escape." I shake my head. "A few more seconds... Who knows what would have happened. I just wish Katie had woken up." I gaze into his eyes with a questioning look on my face like he can give me all the answers that I am looking for, but, of course, he can't. How could he? He combs his fingers through my hair and leans in to kiss me. Slow and soft, taking his time. He pulls away, leaning his forehead against mine.

"I'm so sorry that happened and you lost your friend. I will do everything within my power to help you, and everything I can to find the fuckers that did this," he tells me. My arms tighten around his waist. Pressing a kiss to his shoulder, his scent floats up my nostrils as a single tear escapes and falls down my cheek. I'm getting really fucking tired of these tears, but I just can't seem to stop them.

ELEVEN

Lee

Stepping out from the car, I slide my gun into the back of my suit trousers. The club my dad owns fills my vision in front of me. It's an imposing building that screams of dodgy dealings and illegal activities, but somehow it flies under the radar and is rarely raided. My dad has sent me here to take the pressure off of him and my uncle; it's clear he wants me to take over more of the businesses so he can retire all together, and I don't blame him one little bit. He's getting a bit long in the tooth these days—not quite the man that he once was. Little does he know I have the same thing on my mind every day. I haven't found the right words to tell him that I want out. I want to keep running all of the legitimate businesses, but that's as far as I go. I shake off those thoughts and make my way inside, wandering down the semi-dark hallway to my dad's office.

I hold onto the good times we used to have spending time together as a family. I remember visiting New York City for our first family holiday. Man, I thought it was the bee's knees - I was just five years old and we were going on an adventure. I hang on to those times; I want them back, the free and easy - the simple life.

Life felt good, excitement crackled in the air as I stepped from my dad's car at the airport. The flight was a long one; around seven hours. I thought I was never getting off that plane. This was my dad's idea of a proper family holiday, none of that camping crap over at Butlin's. My mum and dad didn't seem to mind the flight— they were excited, happy and in love. None of us had ever been to America apart from my dad. He had travelled to the States often, but this was my first time ever leaving my hometown. I was so excited I really couldn't stay still for more than five minutes. JFK airport looked huge compared to Manchester with the USA flag flying high and proud above our heads. I thought Manchester airport was big but this was massive. We waited for what felt like years to get our luggage. My dad carried me around on his shoulders; by that point I was so tired yet fighting the urge to give in.

It was crowded in New York—people everywhere, buildings everywhere, noisy, tons of traffic. The hustle and bustle of people was very overwhelming. They drove like maniacs, bright yellow taxis everywhere. It was warm at that time of year. There weren't hills except in the park, and the buildings were huge. I thought of Jack and the Beanstalk and how Jack would be climbing up that building as it reached up into the sky. I had craned my neck wondering if a giant lived up there. I wasn't frightened. It wouldn't matter if there was because my dad would sort him out.

"Baby, look." My mum pointed at the Millennium Broadway Hotel on Times Square, a four-star place right in the heart of the theatre district. My little eyes grew wide at the hustle and bustle around us as I took in the building across the road, all shiny lights and glass towering over me. I was awestruck.

"Wow. I'm hungry, Mum, is it dinner time yet?" My mum smiled and rubbed her nose on mine. I was five, and all I thought about was my next meal.

"Yes it is, baby. Let's go eat."

Once inside, my dad dumped our luggage in the huge hotel room where everything looked big, shiny, and new before ushering us back out to go find some food. The floors I noticed when my mum and dad took my sister and I downstairs were shinier still with black speckled marble underfoot as we walked through the hotel. The walls were a creamy white with huge mirrors on both sides and chandeliers hanging from the ceiling. A thick red carpet crushed beneath our feet as we entered the lobby. They had all types of food including pizza and bagels that everyone seemed to eat there.

The trip was fantastic. My memories are fond, especially of Mum and Dad taking my baby sister and me to see the big green statue of a woman standing tall and proud holding a torch up in the air. My dad told us it had come all the way from France. I wondered how they fit it on the plane because that thing was huge and had to weigh a ton. Mum and Dad laughed when I shared my thoughts with them. I later came to know the green lady as The Statue of Liberty.

I smile at the memory of good days, and quickly, I'm brought back to the here and now. How I yearn to be anywhere but here.

"Mr. Young," my dad's club manager calls out as she greets me, walking into the room with a tray containing a glass and a bottle of Jack. I note the sway of her hips—a provocative walk if ever I'd seen one. I internally roll my eyes, feeling frustrated that she tries every single time I'm here.

"Thanks." I flick my gaze from hers as she sets the tray down on the desk and flutters her long lashes at me, lust clear in her grey eyes. She gives me a kind smile, and I watch her leave the room, she moves her ass a little more and her long blonde hair sits like it's glued to her back—perfectly straight. Not a strand out of place. She can strip naked for all I care; she does nothing to get a rise out of me or my dick.

There's a knock at the door and in comes my uncle Mark, my sister Katerina, and my dad. Alec, my dad's go-to man for just about anything, follows them. He's head of security within all the businesses and has been around since I was born; he's more like family. I pour myself a drink and take a seat next to my dad as I watch everyone else get themselves comfortable. I have never been scared of anything, but right now, at this moment in time, my emotions are running around my body like fucking crack and the nerves are beginning to get the better of me. I need to tell my dad and my family what's going through my head. I need to just lay it out and take whatever my father wants to lay on me. It's now or never, I guess—time to stop acting like a little pussy and grow a backbone here. My sister Katerina is looking just as nervous as I feel which is new. She's always so composed, her emotions tucked firmly aware. I don't know what's got into her lately.

"You know why we're here..." my dad starts to speak, and I throw back my drink at the tone of his voice, and for a little Dutch courage, if I'm being honest with myself.

Surviving You

"About that, Dad—" I try to intervene, but he cuts me off, holding his hand out in front of him in a halting gesture.

"I have signed everything over to you, Son." A deafening silence blankets the room as all eyes land on me, my sister's wide as she stares at me dumbfounded. "You will take over from me, Lee. You pretty much run it all yourself now anyway, all I've done is made it legal."

Katerina is on her feet with an unhappy scowl on her face. "Legal?" she asks incredulously. "You can't make illegal businesses legal, Dad. You do realize what you're saying, don't you? It's ridiculous!" she rants. I stand and raise my hand to shush her hoping to stop her saying something she might regret later. I can see her composure slipping.

"I'm glad everyone's here because I need to talk to you all." I glance around the room. "I want out, Dad. I need to get out. I want to start again, a new life in a new place." I look directly at my father with begging eyes and wait for his reaction. I search his chocolate brown eyes—the same eyes as my own—the corners of them creasing as if he's smiling without his mouth even moving. He knows. He already knows what I want—this isn't news to him.

"What are you talking about, Lee? You can't just leave!" Katerina's voice comes out in a squeaky,

panicked pitch. "Tell him, Dad, there's no leaving. We were born into this—it's our legacy."
"Katerina, shut up and sit the fuck down!" I roar at her. Her eyes go wide, and her lips tighten into a thin line. She's so pissed at me, but my princess of a sister does what I tell her. Now there's a first. "I want my new life in Scotland to be a clean slate. I don't want to take all the shit with me from
here. I need to find out what the fuck is happening with Rose and my friends up there. There's a shit storm brewing, and I need to get to the bottom of it all before something else happens to one of them. There's someone leaking information to these fuckers, someone that's linked to Manchester and in Scotland. I need to find out who." I lay everything out, wearing my heart on my fucking sleeve, watching my dad the whole time with my heart in my throat as I wait for his reaction. This needs to be said, and I need it all fucking sorted. —for Rose, for my friends. I don't want it hanging over them or me like a fucking black cloud. Thinking about Rose, I lose my train of thought and her brown eyes and long, dark, curly hair suddenly take the forefront of my mind. Fuck, I miss her.
"Lee." Bitterness coats my name on my sister's lips like she can read my fucking mind.
I clear my throat and glare at her. "What?" She simply raises her eyebrows at me then looks at my dad. I follow her trail and find my dad grinning at me.
He knows. I'm so fucked, so head-over-fucking-heels in love.

Surviving You

"Well, Lee. Looks like we are both are about to retire," he says smugly.

With that Katerina bounces out of her seat again, throws her hands up in the air, and stomps out of the office. I go to follow her to bring her back to tell her to stop acting like a spoilt brat, but my father stops me, telling me just to let her go for now. She doesn't get it. Why would she? She's been treated like a princess all her life, kept away from all of the shit we have to go through daily, and I wouldn't want her to be involved. Once I was old enough, my dad and I kept her out of that side of things, but she loves the money. She's never had to work a day in her life thus far.

"She'll be fine; I'll talk to her. Don't worry, Lee. Now, then, what about these guys?" Straight to the point, business first, as per fucking usual.

It's been a fantastic three months since I started spending more time with Rose. The best three months of my life by far. However, she's still closed off, keeping up the walls that surround her and building them higher. I don't think she'll ever let me in fully, but it's not for lack of trying on my part. She has a battle going on inside her head; I can see it in her eyes. I see right through her brave face she has for everyone else. I see her fear buried deep down in her soul: A fear of the unknown that I haven't quite worked out how to fix for her yet, but I will in time. I'm not giving up on her. I've never once wanted a woman so much that I crave her every waking hour. Any other guy pays her any attention, and I feel the need to rip off his head. She's mine—nobody else can have her. I need to feel her warm skin against mine, hear her laughter and the look in her eyes she only has for me. I need to make sure she knows she's mine, to claim her and let every fucker know that she belongs to me. Once I get clear of my past, I'm doing just that.

First, I've got this job to do. In the warehouse waiting for Ryan to show up, I shake clear my thoughts of Rose and focus on what's ahead. As I do, Ryan walks in looking like the badass he is in black jeans and a tee, a bandana wrapped around his head, and a huge smirk on his face. His light brown orbs dance. He's fucking crazy, but he's my best friend, like my brother, and I would fight to the death for him.

"Where's your head at? You need to pull it out of your ass. Eejit, we've got work to do." He sits down beside me, a look of concentration clear on his features.

"I'm ready." I nod at him. "Let's do this." He's ready to work, and his expression pulls me out of whatever thoughts I had about Rose. My dad turns up with his team to start going over our plan. One

of the rival gangs in Manchester has a huge house in Hale, a brand new three-million-pound house with maximum security covering every inch, every corner. It won't be an easy job; that's for sure. However, my Uncle Mark can decode any security system in a few seconds and tells us he can do it no problem. I believe him; I'd be a fool not to. I've been on enough jobs with him to know what he can and can't do, but this is a colossal task—one of the biggest and most precarious. With an expensive up-to-date security system, there are cameras covering the place, but he knows he can crack all that while we crack open the safe where the fuckers have got the diamonds from a job my dad did time for. Years ago, they left him to take the sentence that got reduced because the diamonds were never recovered. My dad knew Vince had the diamonds hidden and didn't blame him, but not one of them stepped up to help my dad out or offer to compensate him with half of the cash they'd get for them when he got out. So, he's taking them back, and I'm with him all the way. All's fair in love and war, right

TWELVE

Rose

FIVE MONTHS LATER

The gym is absolutely packed with the usual members and more. I can see the guys through the mass of people because they are by far the sexiest bunch in here. Declan and his brother Logan run side-by-side next to Lee, running fast and hard like their life depended on it on the treadmills in front of the huge mirrors. I can see their concentration as they work hard to push themselves to their limits. Dana and I sweat it out on the cross trainers in a hot guy haze just short of our tongues hanging out, drooling and bugged-out eyes to match. Licking my lips like an animated cartoon character, I wonder if my panting is because of my workout or because of the guys. Not being able to concentrate at all on the task at hand—that being exercise—I tear my eyes away from the sexiest creature in shorts and a tee that I have ever seen in my entire life. God, he's magnificent. I can actually see and taste the lines of his muscles through his damp tee from where I work the cross trainer. I push down my thoughts of Lee being soaked in sweat, sweat that I want to lick off his toned abs. I push all of my thoughts of desire down to the deep depths of my stomach while attempting to drag my jaw off the floor, trying to take my best friend's gaze away from her equally hot man. I give her a playful wink when I catch her attention. Yup, we're both crazy for our guys.

We finish up on the cross trainer then move to the mats for our core work and lunges. Ugh, I absolutely hate doing lunges with a passion, but, unfortunately, it has to be done. Mr. Hotness moves to the weights, and again, I cannot drag my gaze away from Lee working his huge biceps. I don't want to be checking him out right in the middle of the gym, but I am completely entranced, lost in a fog of hazy lust. It isn't until he feels my eyes on him and catches me checking him out do I stop looking at him. My cheeks heat up with the embarrassment of being caught staring at him. He smiles in my direction, a knowing, sexy, all white, toothy smile. *Completely full of himself*, I think. *If he wasn't so freaking hot, I could seriously hate him right now for being such an arrogant ass.* I give him a red-faced glare and he throws his head back and laughs at me. It takes me straight out of embarrassment to oh my God he's stunning to pissed way the hell off at the egotistical pig all in the space of twenty seconds. New record, I'm sure. *So full of himself.* I ask myself again, *why do I let him anywhere near me?*

"Why don't you ask him out? "Dana puffs out as she bends down into another press up. "He's clearly into you, Rose." She looks over at him and smirks.

"Well, I'm not into him." I know I sound petulant, but I'm having a hard time admitting that really I am. "He's an arrogant sod and so full of himself it's damn annoying," I tell her in the mirror in front of me while doing squats, the anger at myself boiling in my veins making me forget the burning in my thighs. I haven't told her yet about what happened the night Katie died. I'm so ashamed of myself for letting him under my skin so easily—that night and ever since. I can't help Mike's voice running laps around my head screaming whore at me. It makes me feel sick to my stomach when I think back.

"Rose, chick, you are so into him too I can see it plain as day. You don't need to hide it from me." She gives me a careful look. "I get why you're scared, but it's time to move forward, time to move on with your life. You can't stay single forever, sweet."

"I am not scared, I just don't like him," I lie to my best friend. She knows I'm lying to her, too. I can't lie for shit, and her smile tells me that she caught me. I can't help but smile back at her anyway.

Single is the safest way to be, so that's what I'll be. Single. Yes, I will.

"Know you are so full of shit, sweetie. DIY and your BOB just isn't going to cut it for you forever, you know." Again with the smirking! This woman reads me like a freaking book. Changing the subject, I ask Dana to come for a much-needed coffee after our workout. Heading for the doors, I give one last longing look to Lee as I leave the guys still doing their thing with the weights.

"Bye, guys." Dana gives Logan a quick kiss on the lips. Waving goodbye, we make our way outside.

My stomach flips as I hear Lee's voice nearing me. I don't slow down just keep on walking quickly, determined to be gone before he catches up. While he is running behind us, I turn my head a bit, hearing his footsteps pound against the ground as he races along. He catches up, and I give him half a smile as he turns in front of me.

"Hi, Lee." He came to a stop, looming over me as he attempts to catch his breath. "Hey, where are going?" I ask Dana as she backs away from us.

"I need to pee," she says as she chuckles.

The last few months, Lee has been chasing after me, paying me so much attention. Everyone has been talking about it. In fact, I bet the entire town is talking about it. I really don't want to be the talk of the town. *It unnerves me.* Hell, he unnerves me.

"Are you embarrassed in front of me?" He tips his head to the side, still looking down at me. Damn, he is so tall. "Don't be, Rose." I give him a small, shy smile. He definitely knows I am a little bit ashamed, but that doesn't stop him from pursuing me. Lee isn't the kind of guy to back down easily. "You're killing me in those gym tights and that tight tank you're wearing."

My face flushing, I realize that, yes, I am embarrassed. He shrugs like it is no big deal with a devilish gleam in his eyes.

"Baby, look at me." I look up into his stunning face and flush some more.

"I'm ashamed, Lee," I whisper. "What we did... It should never have happened. And on the same night I lost my friend."

"Don't think like that. We did nothing wrong, Rose. It was awesome," he corrects me. He dips his head a little, his arm reaching out to catch me as I try to walk away. I find myself being swung around and hold tight against him, a surprised gasp escaping my lips as my hands land on his chest. My skin flushes hotter than it already had from all of the exercise as I tilt my head back to look at him.

"What are you doing, Lee?"

His arm tightens around me when he speaks. "It's been ages since that night, and I'm not cool with not being able to get you alone. It's been too long. So, will you go on a date with me?"

With my hand on his chest, I can feel his heart pounding against my palm. I look up into his eyes. Lord, how I can get lost in them for hours on end.

"Why?" His other arm comes around my waist, and he presses me farther into him. He bends his head, his eyes flaring as my breasts push against his chest. Our lips are inches apart from one another. Just a slight move and we'll be lip-to-lip. I groan quietly at the thought.

Surviving You

"You knocked me on my ass when I met you." I feel his shoulders shrug slightly. "You're smart, funny, and really hot. All I know is that you probably deserve better than me, but I'm too selfish to give up on you. I'm so fucking into you, Rose, you have to know that. I want you to be into me too. Please say you are, baby, put me out of my damn misery." His words send an ache across my chest, firing up my blood, getting my heart racing.

"You're so arrogant, Lee." I give him a light push within his hold.

"I know," he says simply as he chuckles softly and rubs his nose against my own. He caresses the

back of my neck under my hair, sending shivers down my spine as his hand cups my nape, gripping it gently while he dips my head back.

"I'll think about it, Lee. All right?" I half-heartedly concede. "I have so much going on at the moment, but we can do something at some point, I guess." I fidget as I try to catch my breath. I push away from him properly this time, and he lets me go. I feel the loss straight away, and it knocks me off-kilter. Dana comes back along the corridor, so I take my arm in hers and head off to the entrance of the gym. I smile to myself as I feel his eyes burning into my back. I bet he's watching my ass. My smile turns into a snigger that I can't hold in.

We arrive back at our place of work. On the way over, I notice the weather is getting warmer, and it puts a little spring in my step. I love the month of May. Summer is definitely going to make an appearance soon; I can feel the air beginning to warm up around us. We make our way in to get coffee and grab a seat. I wonder how the builders are getting on with the rebuild of my house, and I share this thought with my best friend.

"I'm looking forward to seeing the rebuild. I love you, but I need to get back to normal." I let out a long sigh. "I'm so grateful to you for putting up with me and boo." I take her hand in mine, conveying my gratitude.

Her eyes turn soft as she speaks, "There's no rush; it will take as long as is needed. You and Annie are welcome to stay with us as long as it takes to fix." I love her—she's such a selfless soul.

"I know, thank you. I don't know what we would have done without you. I really appreciate everything you're doing for us."

We sit and sip coffee deciding that tonight we need to work on the care packages for the new women that are coming in the next day. We do this for everyone that comes to us because some come in with only the clothes on their backs and nothing more. It's how I left Mike: the clothes on my back, Annie in my arms, and a backpack with the things I just couldn't lose.

THIRTEEN

Lee

I fell for her the minute my eyes took in that dark, curly-headed beauty. I fell head-fucking-first toward the damn moon. I would run right around the stars, all the way around and back again for her. It would be so easy, but I don't want to let myself feel the way I am feeling for her. I can't. I won't be that selfish. I won't drag someone as beautiful as Rose into the darkness that is me. A depressing, dark, and dangerous world so far underground beneath her. I won't do it; I tell myself again. I don't deserve all that she is. But I am a selfish bastard, and I can't go another day without having her with me. I want to wake up with her beside me in my bed every morning. I want her with me when I close my eyes at night. I want to feel her naked body against my skin, her body covered in my scent. Knowing she's not here with me kills me every fucking day. All I fucking see is her big, brown, beautiful eyes full of fire, passion, and desire for me. Her smile lights up my world whenever I see it on that stunning face, full pink, almost red lips. That curvaceous body, huge tits, and tight little pussy does all kinds of stuff to my throbbing dick. I can't tell her any of this, though, not until I'm sure my family and I are free of the world I grew up in. I would never be able to forgive myself if anything happened to her. But I remember every single detail of what it feels like to have my cock buried inside her. I grimace at the memory of pushing her too far too fast and regret it for a moment. She left after I made love to her and I will never forget the look in her eyes. So full of sorrow and guilt at what we had done. How can I convince her that this is right? That we are right? I catch her watching me in the mirrors in front of me, and it makes my heart swell. Her dark brown hair is pulled back in a ponytail swinging from side to side as she moves, working up a sweat on the cross trainer. Her tight black and pink tank top and gym tights show off every single curve—her ass taunts me. I want to peel her clothes from her body with my teeth and fuck her against the mirrors. Wow, wouldn't that be something? Instead, I run, pushing my feet harder against the tread.

An hour later, I'm thirsty from pounding my legs so hard. I find my bag and grab a bottle of water while scanning the room discreetly for Dana and Rose. My eyes meet the sexiest woman alive and she's checking me out. Her step falters and her cheeks heat to a deep rosy red, the same colour of her sweet lips. Aiming my cocky smile in her direction she gets all pissed off. She's adorable when she's embarrassed and it makes me want her even more. I need to get out of here and take a cold shower before I throw her over my shoulder like the caveman I am and take her in the changing rooms. Make her scream out my name.

I glance around at my friends. Logan lifts weights, concentration clear on his face, listening to the music through his headphones, clearly in a world of his own. Declan pushes hard running on the tread with sweat pouring off his back, so when I notice Rose leaving the gym, I chase after her.

After a cold shower, I dig in my pocket to retrieve my annoying as fuck buzzing phone and swipe at the screen to take the call. "Richie, what can I do you for?" I ask gruffly.

"We need to meet." *What the hell is up now?* Richie never calls unless there is a problem. I tell him where and when and kill the call as I make my way to my car. His calls are never a good thing, and I wonder wearily what kind of shit storm I'm walking into this time.

By the time I get down to Manchester, it's already dark, and the rain is pouring down on me. Never fails. I've never known it to rain so fucking much anywhere. Makes for a somber fucking mood, that's for sure.
I park my Skyliner in the car park, but not before slipping my gun into the top of my jeans since you just never know when you might need or want to shoot someone. I make my way through the doors of my dad's club and find Richie sitting at the bar chatting up the blonde barmaid. He must sense my presence behind him as his whole body stiffens; this makes me hyper-aware that something heavy has gone down with one of our own. Richie turns to me and stands to reach out his hand to greet me then leads me out into the back where we can talk privately.

"What's up, Richie?" I sit myself down in my dad's office chair. Richie's green eyes stare at me as if he's trying to find the right words to tell me what's happened. His square jaw is tense, and his lips form into a thin line showing me that he's angry about something or someone. With that, there's a knock at the door and in walks Ryan looking livid and concerned exactly like I'm feeling.

"Have a seat mate," I tell him. He sits on the edge of my dad's desk. "Well?" Ryan barks.

"Richie!" I snap at him. He lets out a big sigh and sits in the opposite chair facing me, his huge biceps bulging beneath his tee as his hand rubs down his face.

"It's Smithy and your dog, Sniper." The expression on Richie's face is pained, and I ask him again what's going on not really wanting to hear the ugly truth of what's happened to one of my oldest friends and my dog. *What the fucking hell?*

"Richie?" I prompt.

"We found Smithy at home. He had gone AWOL for a few days and by the time we got 'round there, we found him unconscious, beaten so badly we didn't recognize his face." Richie grimaces, clearly remembering the scene. "He was barely breathing, Lee. Whoever this was fucked him up bad and left him to die. They took Sniper. We checked on the CCTV, but all of their faces were covered so we couldn't get anything from that just what they did to Smithy and then taking the dog away."

"Fuck! Why did they target him? Why take Sniper? Any idea who's done this? The fuckers will pay for this when I find out. Is Smithy....?"

"Dead?" he finishes for me. "No. He's in the hospital, and he's not in a good way, but he's still breathing. He's in a coma." I let go of the breath that I had been holding in a sigh of relief that he is still alive, but where the fuck is my dog? I stand up from my seat and start to pace the office floor while racking my brain. Who could have done this and why? We already have a team of people looking into the house fires that nearly killed my friends. Could this be connected in some way?

"This shit is getting out of hand." Ryan is now pacing the office alongside me, his hands running back and forth through his hair. His big, light-brown eyes fill with just as much confusion as my own.

"Get the guys digging deeper into this shit. There must be something to find in all this, and the fires could be connected."

Richie nods, stands, and moves to leave. Before walking out the door, he turns to me. "We'll find these bastards, Lee." And then he is gone, leaving Ryan and me with our own confused thoughts.

Smithy lies in a hospital bed with various bits of tubes sticking out of him, wired up to some kind of machine that beeps. I have no idea what they all mean; I just know my man is in a really bad way. He doesn't look anything like my friend Smithy. The only reason I know it is him is by the tribal tattoo with the word *family* snaking up his forearm to his shoulder and stopping on his broad chest. His face is black and blue. Boy, they fucked him good.

I stay and talk to my old friend for a while hoping that he hears me speaking. I tell him about Rose and Annie. I tell him what I think's happening. I tell him about Ryan trying to shove his dick into any woman that moves. I don't know if he can hear me or not, but I need him to know that I will find the fuckers that did this to him and bring Sniper home again. Lastly, I tell him he is coming home to Scotland with me whether he likes it or not.

FOURTEEN

Rose

"Dana, what do you think?" I stand before my best friend feeling like a million pounds. I'm wearing a floor-length, strapless, cocktail-style dress in midnight black with gold embroidery along the bust that flows down one side to my hip and has a split up my thigh on the other side.

"Rose, you look beautiful. You always do, but tonight you look incredible." Dana stands in front of me with a tear in her eye as she looks across at me.

"OK, no crying tonight, Dana. It's just a dress." She looks beautiful in a long, cream, backless cocktail dress with sparkling diamantes all over it. Her brown, highlighted hair is styled with wavy curls falling down her back. She looks gorgeous. We stare at one another trying not to get too emotional and ruin our makeup.

"Katie would have loved this if she was still with us." She sighs.

"She will be smiling down watching over us. I miss her too, you know." Dana reaches for me, places her hand in mine, and squeezes a little.

"I know you do, Rose. We can party for her like she's still partying with us. She will forever be in our hearts, and nothing takes away the memory of her."

Dana holds one of her hands over her heart as she speaks and smiles a huge smile at me through the mirror. Putting her hand to my heart, she presses firmly. "In here, Rose, always in here." She fixes a lock of my hair that had fallen out of place and picks up the hair spray. "Close your eyes, chick." Closing my eyes tight, she sprays a little more onto my hair.

"There. You're done. You look perfect." My eyes are made up in smoky eye-shadow and my lips a glossy red. I sigh as so much has happened to us in the past few years this feels like a dream. We don't have big parties often, but being Dana's father-in-laws sixtieth birthday, everyone has rallied 'round to throw him a huge party to celebrate. George will be so shocked; we have kept this from him for so long, but he will love it. Despite his age, he's always up for a good party.

"Lee is going to go completely insane when he sees you. You know that, right?" She has that cheeky look in her eyes again. Always the match-maker.

I just don't want to go down that road with Lee. He's a gangster, a player, and I'm scared to trust anyone again. Especially someone like him, but I'm drawn to him. I'm not scared of him—if anything, I feel safe around him. The way he has helped Dana and Logan since I've known him tells me that he's a good man inside and that I will be safe with him. I just can't seem to let go of my past, so I push him away. The way Mike treated me has scarred me for life, and I don't mean just physically, it's physiological too and no matter how much I try I just can't get past it. I know Lee has a past and has felt pain like I have but in other ways. I know he's into some dodgy stuff and has been in that world all of his life. That doesn't bother me but trusting him and having my heart broken does. I see it in his eyes. Deep down in his soul, he's really a good man. But for once in my life, I'm happy. I have to make the best of everything without any complications. I have been given a new life for myself and my baby, Annie. I never want that bubble to burst. Lee has the potential to burst it.

Dana has cracked open a bottle of wine and is pouring us a glass each. "To us!" She raises her glass in the air while handing me mine. I raise my glass the same way and clink it against hers. "To us and being happy. Free and to just live our lives. No more drama." She smiles then takes a sip of her drink. "Oooh, that's good shit, babe."

"Hell yes to being happy and free, girlie. And to living." She throws a warm smile my way when the doorbell rings. Dana goes to answer it, and I down the rest of my wine. Grabbing my purse, I make my way out to the kitchen to place my now-empty glass in the sink. I see it's Logan ready to give us a lift to Lee's. Let the fun begin.

"Did you forget your keys?" Dana asks him. Logan smiles down at her—his adoration pours off of him.

"Yeah I left them in the car; the engine's still running. You two just about ready to go? The kids are already there with Mum and Dad," he tells her.

"They're already there?" We best get a move on then," Dana says.

We arrive at the huge mansion. The gigantic hall leading to Lee's living room is packed out with so many people it's hard to move. Logan and Dana's family members, our friends, Lee's family and friends, and then some. I make my way to the mammoth table that looks like a bar helping myself to a glass of champagne. I search around the room for Annie before spotting her on the dance floor with the other kids. It warms my heart that she's so happy, healthy, and beautiful. Stable, that's what she is, that's what we are. Stable. Not that long ago, things were so unsure for us.

My round, swollen belly had so many layers of protection around my unborn baby girl that for the moment I knew she is utterly safe. A midwife took me aside and told me that, saying she was good and if I ever needed to talk to her I knew where she was. Even while carrying his daughter the beatings never stopped. If anything, they got worse. I had never been so fearful in all my life at the thought of losing my child before she even had a chance to take a breath.

"Why do you have to wind me up and make me hurt you? If anything happens to our baby it's your fault. It's all on you. Stop winding me up all the fucking time, you get me?" My head was down looking at my bump while I tried hard to process his words, all the while listening to him sneer at me. I had to try not to annoy him; I was walking on eggshells as it was. How much more insignificant could I make myself?

"I'm sorry, Mike. I don't mean to annoy you; I swear I don't! My hormones are all over the place at the moment." Begging him like he was my master and I had to obey his every command was really draining the life out of me. I knew if I aggravated him anymore I would pay dearly, so I had to do as I was told or face the consequences.

I look around for Lee, but I don't see him anywhere, and I scold myself for even looking for him. I make my way back over to Dana and take her a glass of bubbly too. The music blasts out from the end of the hall where the DJ sits in the corner. Everyone around me looks so smart tonight. We find a table and pile onto the seats. The conversation soon goes from work to the kids and back to work talk. I'm surrounded by all of my friends and the people in my life that I love and adore, but I feel like the loneliest person in the room until Annie spots me sitting here and comes bounding toward me, jumping up onto my knee to give me the biggest hug and widest smile. It warms my heart further. Regardless of my feelings. I push them aside as everyone is in a great mood, eager to be out for the night and to celebrate. I eventually spy Lee over at the bar. For the occasion, Lee is back in one of his suits. Black, sleek, sharply cut. White shirt with the first button undone, and no tie this time. With his curly black hair and a slight stubble on his chin, he looks good. I want to run my fingers through that hair and down his face. I want to take the suit off and give him something to remember me by. And of course, as I think about this salacious thought, his eyes lock on me, and my cheeks start to burn.

"Rose," he says throatily, his face brightening in awe. "You look beautiful."

He comes toward me with his arms out and grabs me by the shoulders, leaning in to plant a kiss on my cheek. I am so overcome with desire and lust; I feel happy for the first time in ages. I suddenly don't feel so alone. His body so close, his scent making me weak, his lips so soft and warm. My eyes

close as I take it all from him. His greeting lingers when he finally pulls away. I know I'm blushing. He takes his fingers and brushes my hair off my shoulders, smiling down at me gracefully.
"You're the most beautiful woman here. Smoking hot, baby." My skin flushes scarlet. I press my thighs together, squirming in my seat as I do. I notice everyone is watching us, so I clear my throat and sit down to join them.
Melissa, dressed in a tight, short, red, bodycon dress, watches us but swaps the scowl for a smile quickly. So quickly, in fact, I think I must have imagined it. "Look at you two. Aren't you just adorable?" she coos, but it sounds forced. It gets my back up for a second. I give her a confused look because she's such a strange woman.
"Erm, thanks," I say hesitantly.

She draws her lips into a thin line and nods, noticing my uncertainty. After I finish the drink Lee brought me, Lee tugs at my hand and leads the way to the back of the house and into the garden where there are lanterns all lit up, casting shadows across the tables set out for us to have our meal. It looks beautiful, like nothing I have ever seen. And right there and then, for the first time in my life, I finally know what the word romance means.

FIFTEEN

Lee

Wow! There's my beautiful woman, looking absolutely stunning as always. She looks so damn hot in that long, black and gold dress. She takes my breath away every time I see her, making my mouth water. She looks so lost and alone, like she doesn't want to be here, like her head is somewhere else. I want to take her in my arms and drag her upstairs to my bedroom and make her scream out my name while I make her come so hard. Yeah, I could make her look lost in a whole other way. She senses my presence behind her and turns. Looking straight at me, she smiles that big sexy smile reserved just for me. I grab a couple of drinks from the bar before making my way over to her. I can't take my eyes off the most beautiful woman in the room; they bore into her. Taking the drinks back to the table, I sit my ass down in the seat next to her before placing the drink in front of her.

She looks up at me shyly. "Thanks." Her eyes gaze into mine as she takes the drink in her hand and sips at it. That mouth stirs up my cock. Thank god I'm sitting down.

"Anytime."

Dana, Logan, and Declan are sitting next to her with my sister. Mandy and Vicky are sat around the table too, Dana and Rose's friends. They all came up to Scotland together when that tosser Ian found Dana. I can't believe she ever married him; he's a fucking psycho who tried to kidnap her and her kids. I subconsciously shake my head in disgust.

"Dana, how's it going?" I reach down and kiss Dana's cheek giving the guys a chin lift. I've known Dana since I was a kid; we grew up on the same estate together in Manchester. I will do anything for her. She's one of my closet's friends, my sister from another mother, you could say. Logan and Declan are like my brothers nowadays, and I trust them as much as I do Ryan. We have all been through some amount of shit together this past year, and again I would do anything to protect them all. I would die trying to do it. They're my family.

I make eye contact with Rose. She's sipping at her drink and watching Annie smiling, her eyes so full of love and adoration for her daughter. Annie taps the seat next to her gesturing for me to move to sit down beside her when my phone chooses that very moment to ring. Checking the screen, my dad's face fills it. Swiping at it, I answer after I reluctantly excuse myself from the table. I make my way toward the kitchen.

"All right, Dad?" I query.

"Lee, what the fuck are you doing?" "Dad?"

I'm so stunned at my dad's tone of voice; he doesn't speak to me like this. Ever. Something must have rattled his cage something fierce for him to be this way; he sounds so damn angry. I try again. "Dad, what's up?" Nothing... The silence between us is becoming more and more deafening by the second.

"Dad!" I bark out.

"Let me just clear this up with you, son. Which part of don't-shit-on-your-own-doorstep did you not understand?" He pauses as if to punch home the next sentence. "And which part of don't-throw-a- fucking-party-right-after-it-and-draw-attention-to-yourself did you not get?"

I am so fucking confused. My dad isn't making any sense whatsoever. "Dad, what the fuck are you talking about? Nothing's happening near my own house, and you're not making any fucking sense," I shout. I swear he's losing his mind in his old age.

"Son, I will call you back." And with that, he hangs up and is gone. What the fucking hell was that? I make my way back to Rose and the guys, spying Ryan hanging all over my girl. Launching myself, I fling my arm around Ryan's neck and tackle him to the floor. He bursts out laughing as he stares up at me, his sparkling green eyes mocking me. The fucker's goading me. I stretch my hand out to him to pull him up again.

"Keep your hands off. She's mine, mate." Ryan's back up on his feet and in no time he has his arm wrapped around my woman's waist. He laughs loud then waves his hands up in the air smiling like a Cheshire fucking cat at me because he knows that Rose is mine. He would never do that to me. I know he's just fucking with me like he always does—he loves to wind me up. All eyes in the room are on us, but everyone soon realizes we weren't going to kill one another and go back to what they were doing before.

My sister Katerina gives me a quizzical look, her brows creasing together and her nose scrunching up as she pinches her lips together silently asking, "What's up?" She knows it had been my father that had called me a few minutes ago, and I intend to fill her in on it later. Let her know that Dad's finally lost the plot and gone senile. Right now, though, I need to romance my woman. Taking Rose by the hand, I place a kiss on her knuckles while taking Annie's hand in the other. I gaze down at the little girl I've begun to love so much.

"Princess, would you like to dance?"

Annie nods her little head and smiles at me while she curtsies like she's about to dance with a king. My chest puffs out. Rose smiles and winks at me mouthing, "Thank you." I know Annie has had issues with men for a while; she doesn't like men or boys, has big trust issues, and I don't blame her after what her own father has put them both through. If I were her, I wouldn't like or trust me either, but she's slowly coming around. She speaks to me and smiles at me instead of hiding behind her mum whenever I'm around. It's been a long road with both of them. The woman that I'm falling hard for is still fighting her demons inside her head, and this little girl right here has her own demons.

"Annie, after you." She beams up at me as I lead her to the dance floor and scoop her up into my arms and sway to the music. She giggles like the little girl that she is and starts waving her little arms up in the air. Rose is watching me, a sparkling but quizzical look in her liquid brown eyes, like she's searching for something. She's scared to put her trust in me, and I get that, I really do, but there's no way I'm giving up on her or little Annie. My mind flashes back to when Dana and Logan's house was up in flames. I had to leave Rose and Annie to get into that house, but Lord knows I didn't want to. The look in Rose's eyes and the way Annie clung to her was enough to fucking kill me, but I had to. And I would do it again, and again, and again, if I knew that Rose and Annie were safe.

Mid-song, one of my security guys comes running toward me looking to gain my attention. I pop Annie back down on her feet. The gutted look in her eyes kills me. I bend down so I'm down to my knees and eye level with her. "Hey, princess, thank you for the dance. You go and look after your mum for me. I'll be back in two minutes, OK?"

"OK." Annie kisses me on the cheek and runs toward her mum. I'm shocked as shit. It's a small step, but I'm really growing on her, and she on me. My eyes meet Rose's striking brown ones, and I think maybe I'm growing on her too.

I walk into my office and stare at the bank of screens that show different views of my property. I'm not in the least bit surprised to see the police have my house surrounded. The fucking idiots. Do they not know I can see every single fucking one of them? Sighing into my hands, I hit the switch that lights up the front, sides, and back of the house and make my way to the front doors to invite the fuckers in. They can search every nook and cranny in here, but they won't find shit. Maybe they can have a nice cup of tea when they're done.

"Officer." I nod and greet the tall bastard in front of me politely. It's not lost on me the smirk that graces his face as he peers at me.

"Mr. Lee Young?" he questions. "We have a search warrant."

Of course he fucking does, right in the middle of a party. "I thought as much. You do know we are in the middle of a sixtieth birthday party?" He just grins at me. Like he gives a fuck. He's waving his bit of paper in front of my face so I take it from him, screw it up, and throw it at his feet. "Anything gets broken or goes missing, I will personally see to it you don't search anyone's house again. You got me?"

His step falters and fear fills his blue eyes for a few seconds before he steps forward taking his officers into my house with him as I move aside. Making my way back into the big hall, I open the glass doors that lead into the garden at the back of the house and ask everyone to grab a drink and head out the back while the asshole officers do their thing.

"What the fuck is going on, mate?" Logan asks me as Declan, Ryan, and Dana follow him and come to stand by my side looking as confused as I'm feeling right now. I wave my hand in the air letting the DJ know to stop the music for now. This must be linked; someone out there is trying to rattle my cage and so far it's working. Even with the extra security and the guys that I've got. Every available person at my disposal is looking into this trying to find out who's behind all this shit. Why phone the fucking police? I shake my head. It doesn't make any sense whatsoever.

"Your guess is as good as mine. I'll fill you in on what I think is happening after they have finished ransacking the place. But I think everything is linked." I move them out into the back garden because they don't really need to witness this going on. Making my way back into the kitchen, the blue-eyed officer looks shifty. In fact, he looks downright pissed off.

"You won't find anything, I'm clean." I wave my hands around the room. "And as you can see, I'm pretty busy tonight." I smile and grab a bottle of Jack and a glass from the counter. Pouring a large one, I knock it back. "Why don't you go and do some real fucking police work? And start by finding the pricks that put my friend in a coma before I fucking do." My hackles are well and truly up now.

I slide my phone from my suit pocket and place it on the kitchen table and take a seat.

"I'm just doing my job, Mr. Young," he states while he starts having a conversation into his radio, babbling some crap I don't care to listen to.

"I'm sure," I say while pouring myself another drink. It's gonna be a long fucking night.

"We have to follow up every complaint we get." So someone did call it in. The fuckers! With that, Logan and Declan take a seat at the table beside me.

"OK, Mr. Young, we have completed our search and will now leave you to get back to your party,"

"You know where the door is," I reply.

Dana re-enters the room with Ryan, a worried expression on her face. "Everyone's leaving, Lee. Rose has taken Annie home; she didn't want to keep her here with all that going on. We will get going too. I'm so sorry this had to happen tonight." She leans down and kisses me on the cheek. I'm gutted for them. This was meant to be a birthday party, and my life fucked that up. I hang my head in shame as she leaves. Time to put it all on the table.
"Hey, I'm sorry. I was not expecting that. Everything's kinda fucked lately."
I sit at the table for a good hour and tell them the whole sorry story, starting with the fires and my thoughts on the link between everything, about upping all our security even though it's pretty maxed out already, and Smithy, who's never met any of them or even been up here in the Scottish Borders.

Then I tell them about my dog and how I have no clue as to where he was now. I spill my guts, telling it all. Quite frankly, I need their help to find out what the fuck is going on because someone is gunning for me. I'm being targeted. I don't blame Rose and everyone else for leaving. I wouldn't want to be here now either if I were them. Fuck, I don't want to be, and it's my fucking house trashed by the twats searching for fuck knows what.

I unlock my phone and call back my dad and let him know what just happened. I also fill him in on my thoughts about it all and, needless to say, he's not fucking happy about it at all. He's informed me he's going to catch the next plane home.
"I'll see you soon, son."

Sixteen

Rose

I can feel it. Every time the phone rings or the door knocks, the chills run up and down my spine making my heart pound inside my chest. I can sense that I'm being watched. It's so unsettling. Scrutinized by who, I'm not sure, but I've felt it since Katie died. It's making me feel sick to my stomach. The vomit threatening to make its way up my throat. The fear threatening to strangle me.

Bloody hell, how has my life come to this? I had to get out of Lee's house last night; the police turning up like that threw me right off. I know he's into some dodgy shit, but I can't hang around and watch him being carted away by them. I have spent so many years of my life watching my dad being dragged off by the men in blue. Even when he hadn't done a thing wrong they targeted him for anything that went wrong in the town we lived in.

Growing up, my dad was there when it mattered, but he was away more often than not. Away on club business. I had to cut ties from that life. My dad wasn't happy about it at all, but I had to do what was best for me at the time. I have missed him over the years and I often wonder what he's doing now, where he is. I miss him so much right now and I really need him. He doesn't know about Mike. Or anything since. I don't think he even knows I'm in Scotland. But I'm just as stubborn as he is; I won't go begging him to come help me or admit that sometimes I can't cope on my own without him at my back every corner I turn. I'd just end up with a big fat I told you so if I did that. Nope, this is me.

"Hey, gorgeous." I jump out of my skin when Dana approaches me outside the changing rooms of the gym, dragging me from my thoughts of my father. We have just been for a swim and now Dana wants to go over some ideas for our café. "Hey, you ready to go?"

"Yeah… let's go grab a coffee and we can talk," I tell her.

When we arrive at the shop, we go grab a seat. Dana's really excited about her ideas, and I must say I'm pretty impressed by them. The shelter has been the last thing on my mind lately. She's got someone else in mind to help with running day to day things like setting up and maintaining a website, taking the added pressure from us, which would be a Godsend when we are constantly looking over our shoulders.

"Melissa is an old friend of ours from Manchester," she explains. "She was good friends with Lee's sister Katerina; they're still as close now, actually. She has a bit of a thing for Lee, but she's always been like that for as long as I can remember. She's harmless. Lee doesn't see her as anything other than a family friend.

"Logan wants me to be at home more with him and the kids, as you know, and it would be great to spend more time with them, but I also want to spend more time with you and Annie and not just in work." She doesn't even pause for breath. "And, babe, we need to get you sorted out and quick. You aren't living your life anymore. You just exist, keeping the café running, keeping Annie going. What about you, Rose? You are so miserable, and I hate seeing you like this, it's no life to have at all." The love and concern radiating off her when she talks of Logan, her family, and us, shines so brightly around her that it bounces off of her in waves.

"Hey, it's not that bad, lovely. I'm not dead yet." I try and shrug it off like her words don't affect me when they are so close to the truth it slices through my heart like a razor blade.

"Rose…" Her hands cover mine and a single tear slides down my cheek. She knows me so darn well I can't get anything past her. "But you're right; I'm not living. I'm too scared to relax; you know? Look at what happened the last time I got too comfortable: people lost their homes, Katie lost her right to breathe the air we breathe, and she died a horrible death not having a choice to live. I can't get that out of my head, Dana. I feel responsible for her death." I choke out a sob. "What if the person who did all of that comes back again? What if they do something to hurt Annie or you or me?" I frantically shake my head from side to side, tears flowing freely down my face.

"They won't, chick. Nothing bad is going to happen to us!" she tries to reassure. "We have maximum security and we have the guys. They will have to get through all of them first to get to us. Nothing bad is going to happen. You can't live your life like this, Rose. Living in fear of the unknown is taking over your spirit; it's taking everything from you." She's right. I don't want to live or feel like this, always consumed by fear, the not knowing day after day. But somehow I am living each day in a paranoid state. I sense the darkness around me, I feel it in my bones, and I know it's nearby. So close I can feel the breath of evil whispering against my skin, taunting me, watching me, letting me know it never left my side no matter how much I try to run from it.

"There's Melissa now." She nods her head over to the door as it swings shut. "Hey, lovely, come over and meet my friend Rose. I know you've seen each other, but we haven't properly introduced you. That would be my bad." She giggles.

Melissa comes rushing over. She's about five foot five with short brown hair and brown eyes. Quite a pretty thing. She takes a seat at our table and introduces herself. "Nice to meet you. I've heard so much about you. It's nice to *properly* meet you I mean. Not just in passing."

"Nice to meet you too, Melissa." She seems nice. I'm glad we will get more time even just a small break to take the pressure off both Dana and myself. We sit and talk for a while about the Café going over every day details and what Melissa's hours will be. She stands to tell us she will be here first thing tomorrow morning then toddles off to do her thing.

The shop is small. Old-fashioned in a quaint way. It's charming and unique, yet not outdated, but the building is old. The tables and chairs are antique, as is much of the décor. There's a seating area with computers at the back which is the most modern part of the room. We have bookshelves that run along the back wall filled with some of our favourite books along with good old classics. It truly is amazing to see the type of people who just come in for a coffee and a book to read. I love it. It's Dana's and mine, and I can't be prouder of what we've achieved.

Dembie owns the tattoo shop next door. She's an artist and does a mixture of things. She is very talented as well as being very beautiful inside and out. Her drawings and paintings sell for thousands of pounds, but she also loves giving people new ink. She told us she will keep doing it as long as people want it from her. I am so glad it's her that has the shop next door to ours. There's a slight sense of a bit more security. You couldn't ask for anyone as nice as Dembie; she has become such a great friend to both Dana and me.

"Come on, let's go home. I have a bottle of wine with our names on it. We should celebrate." Dana stands and shoves her things into her bag.

I shrug and she giggles as we both make our way to the door. "Wow, you read my mind. That's exactly what I need right now."

We walk out into the car park twittering like a pair of loons. Logan is sitting in his car, and I can see him behind the glass window smiling as he watches us coming toward him. He must have been sitting out here waiting for us for ages to give us a lift home. How sweet.

Once we reach the car, he jumps out. "Your carriage awaits, my ladies." He does a mock bow then opens the passenger side door for Dana to jump in. As she gets herself in her seat, Logan shuts the door and then opens the back one for me. I look out into the road next to the car park at the hectic traffic speeding past; everyone is always in such a hurry nowadays. I wasn't paying all that much attention, but I notice a man in a silver car sat at the other end of the car park. He starts up his car and drives off as soon as my eyes land on him. I get that sick feeling back in my tummy, and the hairs on the back of my neck stand on end as the car cruises past us. I watch it, more curious than ever and see that the driver was wearing a dark hoodie, but I can't get a good look at him. I am more than happy to be in the car now. I had been tempted to walk back home so the fresh air would clear my head, but I changed my mind and took Logan and Dana's offer up on the lift home. Something tells me I made the right decision.

SEVENTEEN

Lee

As soon as she gets back to her new home, I watch her looking around. I can tell she senses that there's something not quite right in here. She scans the space around her then her eyes land on me leaning against the kitchen wall drinking her coffee from one of her new cups. Her curly dark brown hair frames her beautiful but now very angry face. Her brown eyes are blazing with temper. She has them narrowed on me with her hands firmly placed on her hips. Fucking stunning. This woman, even cross at me, makes my cock stand to attention. I don't even try to hide the fact that she has me aroused. My gaze can't help but wander down the length of her shapely curves. I've tasted that body, and I want to taste her again—every single inch of her.

She stands in front of me pursing her lips. "What the hell are you doing in my house, Lee? You have no right to be in here. You do know this is illegal. You can't just break into someone's house." She's seething as she rants at me, her voice shaking and loud.

"I have every right to be here. I wanted to see you, so here I am," I reply sedately, trying to calm her down with the tone in my voice. Really all I want to do is strip her and fuck her so hard on the kitchen counter.

"No, Lee. I don't belong to you," she says, sounding so tired. "You will always be mine," I say with a shrug of my shoulders.

"Lee, listen to me. I'm serious, you can't do this to me." She shakes her head as she looks down at the floor. I stride up to her and lean in toward her so close I can smell her familiar scent, and I breathe it in.

"I came for coffee and to see how you're doing. There's no crime against that, Rose." She's so close I can almost taste her.

"Breaking into someone's house is a crime, Lee, or did you learn something else when you went to gangster's university? Do you need qualifications, or can anyone join?" she seethes. Shit, she really is angry at me.

Her hands are clenched tightly together at her sides as I move in closer still and grab hold of her hips, pulling her in, pinning her to me. My mouth crashes down on her lips, but she pushes me away. I was expecting it, but not the slap I get that stings my cheek like a bitch.

"What the fuck, baby?" I ask, astounded.

"Don't you *baby* me. Get out of my house!" I watch her walk away and open the front door for me to leave. "This thing here is called a door. This is what normal people use when they visit someone's house or property. A door! It's mostly made up of wood," she says in a condescending manner. "You knock on them until somebody opens it."

I follow her to the door while she refuses to lift her head to look at me because if she looks at me she knows she will give in. "They're a fucking obstruction, baby."

Defeated and fucking hurt but glad she is safe in her new home; I walk out leaving behind the only woman I have ever loved. Once I'm outside her house, I give Ryan a call to ask him to watch over her while I'm gone. I need to keep her safe while I try and figure out who's fucking with me. Something's clearly gone wrong, and it's my fuck up. Nobody else's. I didn't notice anything sooner. I'm slipping up somewhere, and it nearly killed Smithy. Whoever it was is sending a message, telling me I'm a fuck up. It's a warning, that they're out for more blood. Of that, I'm sure. I want to be as prepared as I can be. The only blood that will be spilled will be theirs. Slipping my phone back into my jeans pocket, I stalk back toward Rose's front door. Fuck this! She *will* fucking listen to me.

"What are you doing? What could you possibly want now? And I see you listened about the door thing." Opening her front door, she stares at me wide-eyed and looks so fucking hot. Her eyes are filled with lust and anger while she stands before me in just a thin t-shirt. She looks at me as though she wants to fucking devour me and slap me all at the same time. "OK, you need to leave right now. I'm not kidding…" she breathes.
"Leave? Hell no, baby, I'm not leaving so you can try and push me out this time. Not a fucking chance!"
"Lee, can we please talk about this like adults?" Pushing her back inside the house not giving a fuck what she says, I slam the door behind me with my foot.
"Yeah, we can talk after I've devoured every single inch of that pretty little body of yours. You're really quite adorable when you're angry, Rose." Her wide chocolate eyes peer up at me—entrancing me. Fuck.
"Talk? About what?" she asks.
"About us," I say, my gaze never leaving hers. I need her to understand I'm serious about this, about us. I want her. She's not just a fuck, she's everything, and she needs to know that right now. Suddenly she steps in closer to me; she smells like vanilla and it tickles my nose. Her hair hangs down in a mass of curls framing her beautiful face. I wanna tug that hair while I fuck her silly. The thought makes me groan out loud.
"Listen, I don't think this…" I reach out my hands and cup her beautiful face cutting her off. I don't want to talk anymore.

"Don't think, do." I lean forward and kiss her softly on the lips. I can't stop myself. I know I should be staying away from her, but I can't, I want her so damn much. My heart is thumping so hard inside my chest it feels like it might explode. I don't consume her mouth like I really want to. I hold myself back, kissing her oh-so-gently, feeling scared to fucking death in case she pushes me away from her. Timidly, she opens her mouth for me, so I slide my tongue in to meet hers, wrapping my hands around her wrists and pinning them against the wall. I can't hold back anymore and deepen the kiss. My cock has doubled in size and is the hardest I think it's ever been. Sliding my fingers along her neck and breast then down to her hips, I hold on tighter and grind myself against her. I feel her pebbled nipples underneath the t-shirt, and it's only then I realise that she's not wearing a bra. Well, fuck my life. I pull her into me and run my fingers up and down her silky cream skin underneath her top, getting lost in the feel of her warm skin. Shit, I register a knock at the front door, and it drags me screeching back down to earth.

EIGHTEEN

Rose

My head is pounding with all the emotions going on inside my brain. I roll over onto my side to look at the alarm clock.

"Shit," I groan, my eyes popping open as the images from last night invade my mind. "You stupid woman. What were you thinking?" I scream at myself, *I'm such a slut!* Why didn't I put up more of a fight? But then I was saved by a knock at the front door, my Annie, my saving grace in more ways than one. Dembie had brought her back from Disney on Ice in Newcastle—she offered to take her as she was taking her niece. The girls had a ball, spoilt with the show then a sleepover. But Dembie needed her home early as she had to open up shop this morning for a client. Throwing the covers off of me, I jump out of bed in search of Annie; she's already up eating breakfast in the kitchen.

"Hey, baby, you helped yourself?" She grins at me with a mouth full of banana Weetabix.

I worry myself sick about Annie all the time. Katie had become part of our family and Annie had become attached to her. Thinking about the loss of her life that had needlessly been taken away from us just like that with no power to stop it or bring her back makes me remember just how precious life truly is. Her light had been snuffed out forever, but still shines so bright in all of our hearts. I need to get out of here for a while; I need to feed my new addiction. Shopping. I started shopping for clothes, shoes, handbags—spending hours trying on clothes, spending money on stuff Annie and I don't really need, but now she has a wardrobe full of impressive stuff.

Putting on Annie's coat and shoes after she finishes eating, I throw the bowl in the dishwasher. I grab my purse and get Annie strapped into her car seat and drive. Before we go to the metro center, we visit some friends in Berwick who I hadn't seen in a while. It's late afternoon when we finally make it to the centre in Newcastle and Annie falls asleep by the time we reach the blue car park. It feels so nice to get away from the madness that is my life, if only for a short while. Just the two of us.

Climbing out of the car, I open the back door and wake Annie. "We're here, baby." She stretches out her small arms and yawns, trying to open her beautiful brown eyes.

"That was quick, mum." She gives a little yawn as she wakes up fully.

"You slept the whole way so it will seem like no time at all, sweetie. Come on, let's shop and have some fun." She screws up her little nose like she can't be bothered to move but makes her way out of the back of the car anyway. I make sure the car's locked and we head inside the Metro Centre. My phone honks its horn sound at me from inside my hand bag so I fish it out and unlock the screen. There's a text from Lee.

Lee - Where the fuck are you?

OK, someone's not happy, but there's no need for that. I curse and throw the phone back into my handbag ignoring him.

I take Annie by the hand. "Let's go in and have a look then we can grab a milkshake and something to eat after. I'm starving." She smiles up at me, her eyes dancing with mischief. I love this girl with all that I am.

We head over to the ladies and while Annie's in the toilet, I splash my face with some water to refresh myself. Annie comes out and washes her hands then we head back out into the busy Metro Centre. God, I feel tired and we only just got here. I don't understand what I'm doing here with everything that has been happening. Here I am bloody shopping for stuff I don't need. Crazy woman.

Surviving You

We stop just outside Dunes window when I am about to say to Annie we should just grab a milkshake and head home. But the shiny sparkling white killer heels tease me from their shelf in the window display calling my name, begging me to go into the shop and buy them. My bank balance will be royally screwed but hey, I will have a nice pair of shiny new shoes to wear inside the house. Yes, inside the house because I won't be able to afford a night out for a month. I scan the shop doorway; it doesn't look as busy today so I won't be queuing up for bloody half an hour. My sensible head is telling me that I shouldn't be doing this. Why can't I just say no? If I go home empty-handed that will cause my anxiety to sky rocket, but I really do not need more shoes. Take it as a lesson in self- control.

I turn toward Annie and I say, "Chocolate milkshake?" I smile down at her but die inside as I turn my back on the best pair of shoes I've ever seen. Deep breaths, Rose, deep breaths.

"Chocolate milkshake is my favourite! Thank you, Mum," she says in excitement.

Once we have our order and we find a seat, my phone starts going mad in my handbag again. Retrieving it, I am shocked that I have ten missed calls from Lee and three from Dana. What the hell? I ignore Lee's again and call Dana. She answers straight away.

"Where have you been? We've been trying to call you! I've been worried sick, Rose!"

"Why? Annie and I are having some mum and daughter time at the Metro Centre, I need new clothes I haven't bought any since last week," I say.

She lets out a huge sigh, clearly exasperated.

"You do not need new clothes; you have more than one person will ever need. Now listen to me, Lee found out some stuff out about Mike. He's been following us, Rose." I hear a flicker of panic in her voice. "He knows where we all live. Lee thinks he has something to do with what happened to Katie. We don't know if my ex is involved in this, but Mike wasn't alone, Rose, we know that. It seems they have all teamed up together, mine, yours, and the rest of the girls' exes."

"What?" It was all I could bring myself to say. There are no words for what I am feeling right now. Fear creeps in around me, and I put a hand to my throat as I feel that familiar dread clawing through my veins.

"Mum, are you OK? You don't look well. Mum?" Annie tugs at me, pulling my attention toward her.

I put my hand over the receiving end of my phone, getting myself together as best I can before I answer her. "I'm OK, baby, finish your milkshake." Trying hard to keep my voice from breaking in front of my baby girl, I quickly tell Dana I will get home as soon as I can and end the call before placing the phone back inside my handbag.

I look at my beautiful little girl with an enormous ache in my heart. She's been through enough. We have to run again, it's our only option, the only way to put an end to all this suffering. My baby has had so much pain in her life already. I will not stand by and do nothing. I refuse to let her suffer anymore.

"It tastes so good, mum. I love it, thank you." She smiles, totally unaware of the situation.

"You're welcome, sweet," I say, leaning over and softly kissing her forehead.

With that, we finish our drinks and don't even bother to look around any of the shops. I feel sick as the panic inside me starts to take over. The fear is burning through my whole body causing it to shake as that familiar feeling of utter panic, terror, and pain in my chest fills my body. I'm so afraid I struggle to breathe as I search through my handbag for my car keys. It drops to the floor sending the contents scattering out everywhere.

"Shit!" Annie crouches down next to me and helps me to pick it all up again and shove it back

inside my bag. All the hairs on the back of my neck stand up on end, and I swear I feel it again. Someone's watching us. I stand quickly, unlocking the car, moving as fast I can to get us out of here. That familiar feeling of alarm fills my stomach and bile is about to rise up and explode from my mouth any second. Just before I open the car door, a shiver passes over me as a hand lands on my shoulder

NINETEEN

Parking the car, I see her long dark curly hair and long legs that seem to go on for miles. I could pick her out in any crowd. I mentally punch myself in the head for sitting here like a pervert watching her. That smile, those eyes, those tits, and that body. I let out a long frustrated sigh. I jump out of my car, muscles still aching and the adrenaline pumping through my veins from my workout I had earlier, trying to curb my ever-growing rage.

Fuck... I'm nervous. I never get nervous. I reach out and place my hand on her shoulder. It causes her to jump a mile high out of her skin and then fall straight on her ass. *Ouch, shit!*

"I know I'm hot, but there's no need to fall at my feet, baby." I try to make a joke out of it but her big brown eyes send imaginary daggers right into my chest.

"Are you seriously laughing at me?" She's so pissed I almost see the steam coming out of her ears. Her face is a dark shade of red. And I can't stop laughing—even angry she's beautiful. Annie is giggling right along with me. Rose looks toward Annie's happy face and her features soften as she smiles at her daughter.

"I came to find you to make sure you get home safe." Her face is serious now, and she nods looking down to the floor.

"Thank you," she whispers in a barely-there tone.

I reach out to her, my hand brushing against her perfect flawless skin. Her hands are so soft in mine—small and delicate—and it feels like some kind of electricity is pulsing through my body. Like lightning bolts want to shoot right out of my cock with just her touch against my skin. Her large brown eyes look up into mine only they're hooded, sultry as fuck. Her breathing has quickened, her chest is rising and falling as she tries to calm herself down. I can't help but pull her flush to my chest.

Taking her car keys from out of her hand, I open the driver's side door and lead her in. I turn to see Annie beaming up at me as she jumps into the back seat. "You look after your mum. I will be right behind you, OK?" She nods three or four times still with a big grin on her face. She's adorable.

Making sure they're locked up tight inside the car, I climb into mine and start the engine, watching her every move on the road. I'm hyper-aware that she's being watched by those sick little fucks. But I do not want to scare her any more than she already is. It's getting late as we leave Newcastle and head for the little Scottish town we all call home these days. The roads are busy and my grip on the steering wheel threatens to rip the fucker out which would not be good while I'm still driving. I try to focus on the road and on Roses' car at the same time, my muscles are so tense. I do not like this new threat. It's a threat like no other before it, and there have been a lot.

She pulls out onto a winding road. I stick close behind her wishing to fuck I had made them both get in my car instead. I don't scare easy, but this is Rose. She's under my skin, she's in mind, in my dreams. I need her in my bed every fucking night. I want to make it a reality. I know she's mine she just doesn't accept it yet, but she will.

My lights from my car shine brightly in the dark on her tail lights, she seriously needs to get rid of that fucking thing. It's older than I am, but I know she loves that little blue mini. Fighting to catch my breath, my eyes stay glued to her car and the road. I breathe heavily through my nostrils, my heart pounding as thoughts of losing her scramble my mind. We are nearly home, and it's fucking raining, what a surprise. Pushing my car forward, I overtake hers and signal to her through the window to follow me to my house. She is not leaving my sight tonight. Not a fucking chance.

My anger fades as I watch her through the mirrors. She is my calm; she is my Rose. She's my everything. Pulling up outside my house, I jump out of the car and round it to get to her as fast as I can. While she is pulling Annie from the back seat, I slip my arm across her back and take them inside the safety of my walls. We spend the rest of the evening watching movies with Annie on the sofa. Ryan brings us takeout then sits and plays with Annie for a while—a big kid at heart with a huge heart of his own.
But I get it, Ry lost his baby sister years ago, and I know he still blames himself for what had happened, but he was only a young kid himself. He couldn't have stopped it even if he tried. He will make a great dad one day if the asshole stops fucking around and finds himself pussy-whipped. I can't wait until that day comes so he knows exactly how it feels, but more so that he finds what I have found.

Ryan stays over but heads into the security room. Rose puts Annie to bed, and when she comes back she has a glass of wine, automatically cuddling into my side, head on my chest. The need to taste her takes control over me, and I feel like a man possessed as I strip her of her underwear, throwing her knickers on the floor in front of us. Just a small patch of hair when her pussy comes into view on her mound has my mouth watering. Reaching out, I run my fingertip down her slit, making her hips buck. She closes her eyes and releases a long moan. Her eyes open as she watches me remove my tee, her eyes filled with need.

I am so fucking hard. I lick along my lips, reaching down to free my cock from my jeans. I need to be inside her, to hear her call my name. Crawling over her body, I kiss along her stomach up to her breasts, feeling my way through the material. Flipping us over so I am on my back, her warm body sits above me. *God, she looks so beautiful.* Her eyes hooded, her face flushed. I stare into her eyes as she runs the back of her hand down my cheek and neck, a growl escaping from my lips as I watch her hand moving over my chest and stomach. I lift us both up so I'm standing and I carry her to my bed. Rose is *mine* tonight.

TWENTY

Rose

Annie is fast asleep upstairs in one of the millions of bedrooms. I have thrown back three glasses of wine and I'm feeling rather tipsy—rather good. I take the bottle of Jack out of Lee's hand while I'm still cuddled into his side and take a few huge gulps, satisfied with the taste and the burning sensation in the back of my throat. Lee watches me with a blank expression on his face as I stand. Well, fuck him. I decide I am getting shitfaced. I have had the most horrendous day, and I didn't get a thing from the shopping centre. And just like the big bloody so
Annie is fast asleep d can read my mind, he takes the bottle from me, mid-gulp I might add, causing me to sway unsteadily on my feet. I grab it back and with the bottle still attached to my lips, I'm soon crashing straight into a hard chest. Holy Mary Mother of God...
I stare at the bottle after it is long gone from my lips and my grip. "Give that back to me, I was enjoying that," I growl, trying and failing to convince him. Damn. "I said give that back!"

His lips trail a delicate route across my mouth, shutting me up with his tongue swiping over my bottom lip. My body hums to life in delight as my mind argues with my vagina. It want him, boy do I want him, but my mind wants the bottle of Jack back.
"You ass," I whisper shout in his face, and his colossal arms grip me around my waist, hugging me to him.
"Shut the fuck up and kiss me." His lips crash down onto mine, a deep rumble erupting from his chest while his tongue now trickles down the centre of my throat. I'm panting, out of breath, feeling my legs turn as weak as I am on the inside.
"Lee, please...." I'm not sure what I am asking for. His hands ruthlessly torture the swell of my breasts. Moving my hands to his back, he takes hold of them and pins them in the air, fingers wrapping around mine as he deepens the kiss. He moves so swiftly that he is like a ninja in the dark. Before I know what is happening, I am being carried and soon placed back on my feet as quick as he lifted me while his lips are still attached to mine. I can feel my pussy crying out for his cock. Shocks of desire shoot around my body. My hands move to his ass and squeeze the solid globes. Damn, he's fine. His growl fills the silence in the room with the sound of my own heavy breathing.

"Oh, shit..." I breathe as he slides his hands back down my body. When they reach the hem of my t-shirt, he lifts it slowly, torturously above my head and pins my arms to it before it slides from my body holding me in place. My legs hit something. I don't know when we moved, but I find myself pushed back onto the bed—Lee's bed—still caged beneath my t-shirt. My arms are trapped.

I feel Lee above me as his body presses into mine. His breathing quickens as he moves, and I feel his mouth trail kisses down my stomach. The man is slowly torturing me with his tongue and mouth, soft gentle ticklish movements sending shock waves of electricity straight down my spine to between my legs.

"You taste so sweet, baby," his deep voice rasps out onto my stomach. His fingers find their way between my legs to my folds sliding inside me expertly. His experienced tongue swipes at my clit, sucking, flicking like he needs it more than he needs to breathe, and making its way into my core. My back arches off the bed at the sensation—he's killing me. I need his rock hard cock buried deep inside me right now. I try to free my arms and hands from my t-shirt, but his hands grip my arms tight, stopping me from moving them. As I feel his body move over mine, his hips push between my legs and he starts grinding into me. It feels glorious. I am about to come in an explosion before he even gets inside me.

"Lee, oh please," I breathe out into his neck, begging for what, I'm not sure.

"All in good time. You're on fire, like a volcano ready to erupt. I will make your pussy spill out streams of hot lava when I fuck you, baby," he teases with a smile playing on his beautiful lips that takes my breath away.

As if he is peeling back the layers of some exquisite gift, he reveals the black lace of my bra and the soft flesh of my breasts like they are a treasure to him. I soon lose my bra as he undoes the clasp. He runs the tip of his nose down the length of mine; just as slowly his lips and tongue torture my nipple. I drag my nails over the taut muscle; this triggered a deep throaty moan from deep in his throat.

"I need to be buried deep inside you," he groans.

"I need you to fuck me, Lee," I whisper, bringing my mouth to his neck and nipping the skin there between my teeth.

"You are all I will ever need. Two broken souls brought together by fate," he huffs into my hair.

"Lee!" I gasp desperately for him to hurry the hell up.

"Please, Lee," I'm begging him to take me now. I'm feeling like such a wanton whore.

His fingers stroke along the side of my face and my jaw, his eyes following the path his fingers just made. "You are so beautiful, I could look at you all day," he whispers, gently pressing his lips to mine. My t-shirt feels tighter around my arms toward my wrists. His hands move over mine so I can feel his thumbs and fingers stroking my skin through the material. I'm pinned against the mattress; there's no escape. I have no intentions of escaping this man. His teeth sink into his bottom lip, and his eyes light up with fire and lust. My eyes are mirroring his.
"Turn over," he orders in a soft tone.
I try to turn my body around, my t-shirt making it almost impossible. I try again to remove the "material handcuffs" so I can at least get one hand free and move a bit quicker. I must be too slow for him because he deftly flips me over onto my stomach before I could say Bob's your uncle. My face is squashed against the soft pillows and Lee's warm breath is blowing on my neck as his lips move to my ear where he whispers; "I'm gonna make you scream my name so loud, baby. And make you come like you've never come before." His voice is husky and teasing.

"Lee, just take me. Please! You're killing me." As if he had been waiting for me to invite him, he slams his thick, rock hard cock into my entrance. I'm so wet that I hardly feel the pinch of pain. He sucks in large breaths as he thrusts in and out of me, over and over, strengthening my building orgasm, taking me higher and higher as he builds up his own. His rhythm is not only hypnotic but the most erotic I have ever had in my entire life as he continues his assault on my pussy. He has me crying out in deliria it feels so good.

He squints his eyes and seems to be studying me, his warm breath whispering across my skin. "I will always be the lost boy you saw that night through your aunt's bedroom window. He's still in here somewhere. I just need to find him, baby, I'm not lost entirely. My soul is yours. My heart belongs to you…always."

My mind is completely oblivious to his words. I have no idea what he is talking about right now. He could be my anything—blue skin with red hair—the way he is making feel right at this moment. I wouldn't give a damn if my dad rocks back up in my life. Instantly, the thought spooks me. My body arches, and I push him off me, rolling onto my front. I sit up straight in alarm. My back would be touching the ceiling if it got any straighter. Why the hell did I think of my dad? Jesus Christ talk about killing the moment. *Dad, get out of my head, go back to your God damn Harley and your crew, and*

please leave me the hell alone.

Surviving You

"What's wrong, baby?" Lee sits up next to me, his lazy eyes blazing concern.

"Nothing, I'm OK." I touch his cheek with my hand and stroke his cheek bone with my thumb, hoping he can't see right through the lie.

"Did I hurt you?" he asks with a worried expression on his face.

"No. No, you didn't hurt me I swear, just stupid thoughts—my dad popped into my head," I confess.

"Your dad? Fucking hell, Rose." Yeah, he's not impressed, and I can't say I blame him. "You need to chill and stop thinking so much. Switch it off." He's right, of course, and the look on his face, the kind of look where I know he's pissed, slays me. I'm pissed at myself for even letting my thoughts stray from him after what we just did.

"Listen, I'm sorry. One minute I was in the moment then the next the thought was just there."

Moving my hand down his back in a circular motion, I trace the length of his spine followed by my lips tracing kisses down and back up, loving the feel of his hot skin under my lips. His back loosens, and I feel him relax under my touch, a moan escaping his lips. *God, I need this man, I really need him.*

He thrusts hard into me, my walls gripping like a vice around his hard cock. As our bodies slap together with each thrust, I cry out his name.

He grips onto my hips pushing hard in our frenzied fucking. I push my ass back against him encouraging him to fuck me even harder.

The heat spreads through my body, travelling through me, racing for release. My walls tighten, gripping harder. His hot come fills me up as I come along with him. Arching my back then collapsing on the bed, he falls on top of me and strokes my sweat-covered hair while our breathing slows to a normal rhythm.
"I love you, baby," he whispers. *"I love you, Lee."*

TWENTY-ONE

Lee

"What the fuck, Lee?" *Christ, not even a fucking hello.*

My dad is way pissed off, and all I can do is stare at him with a confused as fuck expression on my face when he climbs into the passenger seat of my car. He just got off the plane. I've been waiting for over an hour for him at the airport to give him a lift home to Manchester. He's still in holiday mode, dressed in white three-quarter-lengths and a white shirt and man flip-flops.

"Dad. you didn't need to fly back over here! I've got everything under control. I've got this." "Like fuck you have," he growls. "You've been pussy-whipped so bad by that bitch that your brain is attached to your fucking dick. Sort your fucking head out."

Bitch? He called her a fucking bitch. My fists clench tightly together while I try my fucking hardest not to knock him the fuck out. My own dad.

"Show a bit of fucking respect, Dad. She's no bitch, all right? And her name is Rose." I put a long, loud emphasis on the name, eyeballing him.

"Exactly, what did I just say? Pussy-whipped. Holy fucking shit," he shouts out,
My dad is now ranting, mostly to himself, beside me. I decide the best course of action is to ignore his ranting fucking face. I swear in all my years I have never hit my dad and never wanted to until now. Nobody disrespects my woman, not even him. I put my foot down wanting to drop his ass off at his house as soon as fucking humanly possible.
"So tell me, Lee, what the fuck's been happening? Smithy? Sniper? Have you found him yet? I know about the shit in Scotland, but who's this guy your sister's been seeing?" What the fuck? Now there's something I don't know, and that makes me uneasy. Katerina never usually hides things like this from me.
"What guy? I have no idea. As far as I know, she isn't seeing anyone. Probably some poor guy from the club she's picked up. She's not the good little princess you think she is, Dad. Melissa is back on the scene working in the café so they would have been out on the prowl. You know what they're like when they get together."
"Fuck." Truth hurts.
"So you mean to tell me you blame me for my sister shagging some random guy? And you have flown so many thousands of miles to tell me that?" I ask, shaking my head in disbelief.
"No, we have business to attend to that I can help with." I laugh a little. Yeah, he can't keep away. "So much for retiring, Dad," I scoff. Finally, he smiles.

"Where are you going once you drop me off?" My dad rubs his hands on his knees; he hates being a passenger, and I can see his anxiety in the way he's sitting.

"I'm off to see Smithy, see how he's doing. I haven't been to see him in a few days. Do you want to come for a visit? To be honest I'm running out of things to say to him. It's been months, and I'm thinking he could use some other company besides me. He must be sick and tired of listening to me droning on in his ears by now." He stares out of the passenger window at the traffic rolling by. I can tell he's mulling over what I just said.

He's known Smithy since he was born; his dad was my dad's best friend back in the day. He was murdered with his wife while they slept in their bed. Smithy was four years old at the time, asleep in his bed in the next room when it happened. My dad's never gotten over the terrible tragedy, but he made sure they paid for what they did. He hunted the fuckers down then tortured and killed them slowly for what they had done to his best friend, someone he called his family. Turns out they had been robbing their house. Junkies looking for a quick fix. They chose the wrong house and things turned ugly fast since Uncle Johnny, as we used to call him, and his wife had been out that night to a wedding reception; they had both had a lot to drink. My Uncle Johnny tried with everything he had to fight them off, but they shredded his chest. Within seconds, it was wide open with a meat cleaver. Then they slit his wife's throat because she wouldn't stop screaming. The neighbours had called the police because they could hear her screams. "It was like someone's being murdered," is how they described it to the phone operator that took the call. But by the time the time the police had shown up, the junkies were long gone leaving a trail of destruction and blood-covered walls behind them. It was horrific, and I know my dad still suffers the occasional bad dream because of it.

"Yeah, son." He sighs. "Let's go see young Smithy."

Surviving You

Pulling my Skyliner up in the car park at Manchester Royal Infirmary, Dad has gone eerily quiet, clearly lost in the past. I think I prefer it when he's ranting at me; he's never been any good at the emotional stuff. He loves Smithy like a son. He's always looked out for him growing up, making sure he was well taken care of, giving his Aunt money, taking him on holiday with us every year. He spent more time at my house than at home.

Smithy is lying motionless in that bed looking like he's having the best sleep he's ever had. My dad leans over him with a pained look on his features. I can tell it hurts him to see Smithy like this.

"I'm going to get a coffee. Do you want one, Dad?" I ask, but I don't think he hears me. I will pick him one up anyway. I make my way out of the private room of the intensive care ward, into the halls, leaving my dad to spend time with my brother.

While I stand in the queue impatiently waiting for the line to go down so I can pay for our coffees, my phone buzzes in my jeans pocket. "Who the fuck is this now?" I curse under my breath.

"What?" I snap.

"Lee, it's Ry. Guess what I managed to catch last night?" I don't want to know about his latest whore, and I tell him as much.

"Ry, I'm kind of busy, mate."

"Well, listen up. Get yourself unfucking busy and get your ass over here pronto before I shoot this fucker without you. I'm itching to pull the motherfucking trigger or slice him up with my favourite blade."

"On my way." That's all he needs to say to me to get me moving. Running back to Smithy's room, I let my dad know the score and make my way out to the old building.

"What you got?" I growl at my brother as Ryan wipes his sleeve across his bloodied head.

"I got a lock on this fucking prick when I talked with Rose about her ex-man. I didn't find the fucker, but I checked the security tapes again and spotted this tosser's tattoo. Did some research about ex-police, the only few that have these tats. Easy to find, mate." He smirks at me like he just won the fucking lottery.

Sitting before me on the dusty old floor is a man, his head covered with a fucking sack tied around his neck, tied at the ankles with rope, and his wrists tied in front of him. His head shakes from side to side as his back hits the wall.

"You went after him on your own?" He just stared at me not uttering a word. "I'm gonna kick your ass for this. What were you thinking?"

Ryan runs his hand down his neck. "This is the knob that killed your woman's best friend. He's the one I saw throwing the petrol bomb into her kitchen window. It's on security footage."

I crouch down before the man at my feet pulling the sack from his face seeing his mouth gagged with a piece of rope. "Fuck..." I hiss through gritted teeth. My hands start fidgeting, my fists clenched so tight, my nails digging into the skin of my palms so hard that I draw blood.

Ry flicks his narrowed eyes to me and he spits. "He's mine," he growls. He is now pacing the floor thirsty for blood. He's a sick motherfucker, but I need him to have my back, and mine his.

"He's yours, mate," I say while staring into the man that murdered Katie. "Make it quick, none of that slow slicing fucked up shit you like." The thought makes me cringe.

"Your boys aren't too smart leaving a trail a mile fucking long. Dumb fucks." Ryan hisses at the man with long hair and a beard. Ry paces with a sharp knife in his hands, running his finger up and down its blade. The guy makes a muffled sound trying to talk through his gag. Ry comes and sits on an old wooden stool beside him and leans back, staring at the scum before us. I stand against the wall just watching as the dickhead meets my hard stare. Then he swallows hard. I grin.

"Pussy! Not so fucking hard when you're faced with the threat of a man, now are you? Just like killing innocent women, huh?" Yes, a total pussy.

"So, it seems you have been a bad boy, haven't you?" Ryan grins over at me. "Who are you working with? Like we don't fucking know already, but I'd like to hear it from you." Ryan asks while removing the cunt's gag.

"I've got a shit load of money stashed away; I can give it to you—all of it." The man stammers. "How much do you want?"

Ryan laughs with his eyebrows raised. "We don't need your fucking money, you prick. We have plenty. We need fucking justice." Ryan jerks his chin to me. I waltz over to the other side and lift up the scruffy-looking man by his throat, pinning him high against the brick wall.

"Please don't kill me. I'll tell you what you want to know!" He screeches, his words barely comprehensible through my tight grip. When his face turns blue, I drop his skinny ass to the cold dirt floor.

"Tell us who are you working with." His face pales at Ryan's demands, the guy realising he is in a no-win situation.

"I don't know everything. Just Mike. I just know Mike." He ushers the words quickly. I see red and fly at him again, barely containing my anger. The scrawny fucker pushes out his hands, screaming and scrambling up against the wall.

"OK, OK, fuck!" he screams. I pull myself off.

"What?" Ryan snaps. Moving back in front of him, he shouts, "You better start fucking talking; I don't have patience for this bullshit coming out of your puny mouth, you Eejit."

I throw back my head and laugh at my brother itching to slice this motherfucker into tiny pieces. The cunt on the floor rubs his head with his tied hands in obvious fear. I start rolling my neck and cracking my knuckles, my patience wearing pretty thin also. I jerk my chin, ordering the man to start talking.

"The order came from Mike, that's all I know. I swear I'm telling you all I know. I am telling you the truth," he begs, his face turning red, the sweat pouring off him.
"Where's the location of their base? Where the fuck are they based?" I boom in his face.
"I don't know," he stammers. I look toward Ryan, lifting my chin to tell him that's all we're gonna get.
"No fucking about, Ry." I stand up, giving one last look at the sorry excuse for a man sitting slumped on the floor, and then I walk away.

Twenty-Two

Rose

I stare at my reflection in the mammoth floor-to-ceiling mirror in the bathroom inside one of Lee's clubs. It's a beautiful bathroom; modern with a marble counter and built-in sinks but no windows. Am I really going to do this, put myself out there? It's like putting the mouse among a crew of hungry cats, the extraordinary and high-end world and the unlawful world all in one place. Club Liquid is a place where the very rich and sometimes famous people like to hang out; definitely not my idea of fun. And not just the rich you might think of but the hardened criminal rich mixed in. The fact that these two types of people rubbed shoulders regularly makes me laugh.

Surviving You

After trying on five other dresses, then also contemplating trousers and a nice top instead of showing a bit of skin at one point, I changed my mind back to a dress. It looks good, but it's not my usual dress code. It's nude with thin straps over my shoulders and sits farther on my thighs than I would like it to. Relatively classy, not slutty in the least. High nude heels to match, of course. It's a huge transformation from my comfy Jeans and t-shirt and the faithful, old Converse I wear on a daily basis. The lights make the dress sparkle making me feel like a trillion pounds. I like the dress very much even if it isn't me.

Music booms through the building as I reapply my lip gloss in the mirror when the door to the bathroom opens. A tall, skinny, big-busted woman walks in, her nose sky high, her platinum blonde hair straight as a ruler and her lips a bright pink. *She needs to go home and put some clothes on*, is what I think as I take her in. *She looks out of place.* I catch sight of her shorts that look more like a thong, and a bikini top I can see her nipples through. *Christ.* And here's me, worried about what I look like. She fixes her lipstick in the mirror, turns toward me when she's done and looks me up and down, drinking me in from head-to-toe. I can feel her razor-sharp daggers shooting at me, and then she twirls around on her heels with her nose turned up in the air again like her shit don't stink the same as mine before she makes her way back out into the club, the music bellowing through the door. Well, fuck...

I turn back toward the mirror and run my fingers through my dark curls. I shake my head since it looks fine.

Lee walks into the bathroom a moment later not caring at all that it's the ladies. I guess it's his club so he can go wherever he pleases. He looks so handsome in his suit trousers and shirt that I pause to appreciate his broad shoulders. The top buttons of his shirt are undone, showing off the dip of his throat. He has a slight stubble along his jaw, his hair in that tangled mess. He stops dead behind me, sucking in a sharp breath, slipping his huge arms around my waist, his hands warm and soft resting against my stomach. I feel the heat through the thin material. His eyes gaze at my reflection in the floor-to-ceiling mirror full of longing and desire, his head resting on the top of mine, locked eye-to-eye. I smile and press my head into his chest. This all feels so right, this moment.

"You look beautiful," he breathes into my ear as his eyes travel the length of my body then back up to meet my eyes again. His hand takes hold of mine. Slowly, he pulls my arm up in the air to rest on his shoulder, his fingers sweeping down the inside of my arm.

"Mmm…" I moan.

"Where's your jacket?" he asks in a low voice as my eyes fly open.

"Why do I need a jacket when it's so hot in here?" His hand strokes slow feather-light circles down the side of my breast, eliciting another moan from the depths of me.

"I don't want anyone else looking at you, baby." His voice breaks a little. With hooded eyes, he kisses my temple and continues to torture me, his other hand pulling my other arm up to rest on his shoulder, his fingers travelling down the exact same way as he had done on the other. His erection presses into my back, growing by the second. I turn around and run my hands up his shirt. He grabs my hips, his fingers digging into my skin. I reach up and kiss his soft full lips, and his tongue slips into my mouth. Pressing himself against me, I reach my hands up his shirt with my fingers pressing into his lean muscles. The noise he makes from my touch makes me smile against his lips.

Twenty-Three

Lee

"Jesus, baby, you're killing me. I'll be taking you home early if you keep that up. Shit," I say slightly pained, my cock expanding inside my boxers as my hands sweep down her soft body. I reach the hem of her dress and run my fingertips up her thighs. Her breathing has become rapid as she moans into my neck, her soft lips trailing along my skin telling me just how much she wants me.

"I want to see what you do here. As much as I want you to take me home, I'd love to see how the other half live," Rose breathes into my ear with a husky voice.

"Its businessmen, players, and all kinds of entrepreneurs, baby. Boring. In there they are networking mostly to see who's got the biggest dick." I laugh as she stares at me wide-eyed. Of course, they enjoy themselves and have fun, but work never stops.

"Really? Where's the fun in that?" She flashes that beautiful smile at me, her arms moving to rest her hands at the back of my neck.

Her forehead rests on mine as I ask, "What do you call having fun, baby? I know how much fun we could have right now." My tongue lightly grazes her ear. She shudders at the contact, my lips ghosting down her neck.

"We could have all kinds of fun, but this is a public bathroom," she says, her hand palm side up waving around the room.

"It is," I say, running my hand underneath the hem of her dress, pressing against her damp lace knickers between her legs. "But it's mine, as are you." Her eyes close, and she lets out a low moan as my fingers move in slow circles around her clit. A knock sounds at the door. Her eyes fly open at the sound yet she smiles against my lips.

Fixing her dress, she says, "Let's go and network then."

I have my girl on my arm and a troubled mind, but I am glad she is at my side. It can't get much better than this. I feel like the luckiest man alive. We dance to the music, and if I could have made her wear a coat and a hat to cover that stunning body all night, then I would have. The rage I feel inside me is bubbling as all male eyes in my club are trained on my woman. I suck it up, having no choice other than to keep myself under control in a room full of testosterone. When I catch sight of how happy she looks and how beautiful she is, it calms my rage until she is all I can see. I fail to keep my dick from growing hard every time she grinds against me. We spend the rest of the night laughing and enjoying one another's company. The night ends, and she stays over at my house as I have decided to take her out again the next day. I want to spend every waking moment possible with my girl. And that is exactly what I am going to do.

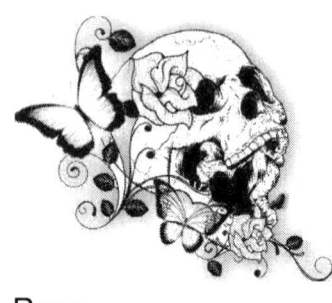

Twenty-Four

Rose

Lee and I walk hand in hand along the high street. "I'm starving," I complain.

"I thought you would be, so it's a good job I booked us a table for some dinner," he says, smiling down at me.

"You did?" I ask.

"I did." There's that smile again, the one that makes me go weak at the knees. Every single time. "A little Italian place just up here." He points to the end of the high street in the direction of the old Castle Jail sitting proudly on a small hill. "I wanted to take you somewhere nice; I want to spoil you. Logan's dad recommended this place. I told him we were coming into town, and I wanted somewhere nice to take you because I've been away, and I feel like I've hardly seen you. It feels like we've been apart for too long."

"Thank you." I grin up at him, his brown eyes turning a shade lighter as the sunlight hits them. He's so beautiful.

"No need to say thanks. You deserve to be treated like a princess," he replies as he pulls my hand up to his mouth, pressing a gentle kiss on the top. We stop just before the Castle gates, and his eyes meet mine. He takes hold of both of my hands and he kisses me gently on the lips, and then he leads me to the restaurant door and opens it for me. We walk into the reception area, and we are shown to our table by the window. The restaurant is small, decorated in light modern colours with romantic lights all around the space on the walls. It has dark wooden beams across the ceiling. It's warm and inviting—a cosy ambience.

After eating a mountain of food and downing a couple of drinks, we make our way outside. We walk toward the ancient Castle Jail, and I catch that mischievous look in Lee's eyes. I know exactly what he is thinking just looking at him; he takes my hand and proceeds to pull me toward the entrance to the Castle.

"No, no....no way I'm going in there, Lee. It's dark," I whine. It has started to get dark now, and I panic a little at the thought of going inside the spooky and supposedly haunted jail. I've only ever been in with Annie during the day, and that was bad enough. There's something about it, and even though it's old and spooky and supposedly haunted, it looks so beautiful all lit up against the dark night sky. It is said to be haunted by an old prisoner who had been executed in the eighteen hundreds. It's said he has threatened members of the public. This thought doesn't fill me with much confidence yet I giggle as we run together through the doors and make our way inside. I am met by the dark eerie atmosphere. Lee doesn't seem fazed at all by it as he leads me down a dark stone staircase and into a dimly-lit hallway. The cell doors in front of us are wide open. I find myself pressing farther and farther into Lee's armpit, his huge arm pulling me in tighter like he senses my fear. My protective shield against whatever might be lurking in the shadows.

I shiver. "Nothing's going to happen to you, baby. It's not the dead you should fear but the living. Not some ancient assed ghost." He smiles reassuringly. Suddenly, there is a loud crashing sound to our right. Fuck. I jump out of my skin with fright; we both freeze where we stand at the noise.

Like lightning, Lee is pushing me backward into one of the cells. "Shhh, stay here," he mouths as he starts to walk slowly down the hallway.

There is no way in hell I am staying put in this old cell with a female prisoner staring at the cell wall, even if she is a dummy, so I slowly move to the door leaving her behind to stare into space. I follow Lee back the way we came. I came to a stop at the end of the hall, and I jump at more loud banging and crashes. I start running as fast I can, struggling to get my legs to move fast enough, fear gripping every part of my body and soul. Where is he? I run down the old, stone, narrow staircase, my adrenaline pumping through me. I run through the reception area where a man had been sitting behind the counter when we arrived. I lean over, and the same man is now crouched down hiding, shivering, and shaking—gripped by fear. I push away from the counter, and I run as fast as my feet can carry me. The sight before me when I reach outside the Castle Jail is horrific. It brings me to my knees instantly. I sit on my heels, and I call out to him. "Lee!" He is crouched down on the ground holding someone, a boy; he can't be more than seventeen. "Lee," I call out again, my voice breaking. But he doesn't speak, doesn't look at me, he just sits there on the grass holding the boy in his arms staring down at him. He is covered in blood.

Suddenly Ryan appeared in front of me. "What the fuck?"

I stare at him blankly. "I.... I don't know.... I just found him like this," I say. I look down at Lee again and watch as his fingers gently close the young boy's eyes.

Surviving You

Ryan crouches down beside him, his arm wrapping around his shoulder. In a soft Irish voice, he asks, "Mate, what the fuck happened here?"
Lee turns his head toward Ryan as he speaks. "Gangland killing. He's just a fucking kid. These guys stabbed him about twenty times. I couldn't stop them. By the time I got out here, they had dropped him and ran off." Ryan stands and pulls out his phone to call someone just as the police are arriving. Just as my beautiful meal makes an appearance in the grass beside me.

"Dana, Rose, my darlings! You both look so sweet tonight. I love your hair, Dana, and Rose, you look fantastic of course, with all your naturally curly hair. I always wanted your type of hair. You're so lucky, sweetheart. And with that beautiful face and a body to die for." She clucks her tongue in appreciation. "You must have men queuing up at your front door wanting to take you out on a date. And Dana, sweetheart, look at you; haven't you grown into quite an adorable woman." I swear this woman is lovely, and I know she is Lee's sister's best friend, but if she calls me sweet or sweetheart *one more time* I can't be held responsible for my actions.

"Thank you," I say simply. I mean really, what else is there to say?

"Now, Dana, tell me all the gossip about Lee." I watch the smirk cross her face, and it confuses me for a moment. "How is he really doing? What has he been doing while I haven't been around? I have seen him a couple of times since I've been here but just in passing. Boy, he looks just as hot as I remember him." *She mock fans herself*, and I roll my eyes discreetly. *Seriously?*

"He's doing great, Melissa. He's a successful businessman. Oh, here's the barman." She waves her hand at the bottles behind him. "Two Jack and Cokes and two vodkas and Cokes please," Dana shouts across the bar. I can see the relief cross her features when the music blasts around us drowning out Melissa's voice.

Katerina sits on the bar stool next to me, and she asks, "Hey, Rose, how's everything with you?

We haven't spoken properly in ages."

I turn and face her not really in the mood to socialise and not wanting to be rude either. "Things are good. Same old same old, you know. Nothing much has changed, chick." Retrieving my buzzing phone from my bag, I check the caller ID before I get the chance to ask her how she's doing. Private number. "I don't think so." I ignore it and throw it back in my bag. But the persistent asshole keeps calling me.

"Hey, ladies, let's find a table." I help Dana with our drinks, and we all sit down at a table in the far corner.

I knock back my drink without realising how much I needed it. After the week we have all had, I needed to be around my girls. Lee has been so quiet after that night. Ryan has told me he's good and more determined than ever to leave that life behind him. I will never forget the heartbroken look on his face or the sight of that poor boy, his life taken in a split second, and for being related to someone from a street gang in Glasgow. Guilty by association. That shit sucks right there.

"Shots!" Melissa shouts. "Let's do shots. You up for it, Rose?" Melissa's wide smile makes me giggle, and I relent; I haven't had a proper girlie night out for ages, and I intend to make the most of it. The Cole House is a bar not too far from Lee's place. They host live bands at the weekends, the place really coming alive with a cool, vibrant crowd. "So how are you, Waff?" I ask Katerina, using

the name everyone else seems to call her.

"I'm really good, thanks, Rose. It's good to see you. It's been too bloody long." She smiles, picks up her shot Melissa had just placed on the table in front of us, and throws it down her throat. Out of nowhere, she throws her arms around me, hugging me tight. Hugging her back, I tell her it's great to see her too. Dana approaches with Dembie; she has been to the ladies and bought another round of shots on her way back. *Crikey, I better get this one down!* Throwing it back, it slides beautifully down my throat and warms me up inside.

"Wow, that stuff will put hairs on your chest." I kind of have to shout so she can hear me. Dana laughs a full-on belly laugh, and I join her.

"Might be a good thing, that. Keep the nipples warm in winter," she shouts in my ear.

"Yeah, wouldn't have to worry about smuggling peanuts anymore." We sit and giggle while the alcohol takes hold.

Dembie brings more shots and *oh my God* she looks absolutely stunning. I take her in as she walks across to our table. I love this woman; she's from Newcastle and the most down-to-earth girl you will ever meet in your life. So talented. So lucky to call this lady my friend. I go all mushy at the thought of these women that hold such a beautiful place in my heart.

Dana grabs my hand and pulls me onto the dance floor where we spend the next couple of hours getting lost to the music and drinking our weight in alcohol. By two AM, we are all hanging onto to each other in the hopes of not falling on our asses, and singing on our walk home. Lee's house is the closest from Jedburgh town centre, so we all decide to gate-crash his place and use the toilet because I am desperate for the toilet.

"Bloody hell, ladies, I'm bursting. I really need to pee!" I shout while hanging onto Dana's arm while we sway backwards and forwards in a zigzag. We must look crazy.

"Do not pee your knickers. It's not a good look, Rose! I know Lee likes you wet and hot but I don't think he's into golden showers, my love." Dana grins. The bitch bursts out laughing too which makes me laugh and need the toilet more. She *so* did that on purpose. I can hear the rest of the girls all laughing behind us.

We make it to Lee's front door which is all lit up. So much so it is harder to see the doorbell. On my third attempt at ringing the doorbell, the front door flies open and beautiful Lee stands before us with a stupid grin on his face. Ryan comes up behind us; he must have been our babysitter for the night. Funny, I didn't see him anywhere.

"You got this, mate? I've got shit to do." Lee nods, and I wonder what he could possibly be doing at half two in the morning. Ryan disappears into the dark night, and I think nothing more of him.

"Let me in," I slur drunkenly. "I need to pee, as in right now." Falling forward through the front door, I run toward the bathroom, stumbling as I go.

As I make my way back down the hallway, holding myself up against the wall, I might add. I

follow the sound of laughing voices to the kitchen where I find everyone sitting around the table. "Better?" Dana smiles and taps the seat next to her where I manage to sit down without falling.

Yay, go me!

Dembie, Melissa, and Waff are discussing holidays, but my mind isn't really paying attention. Lee sits down in the empty seat next to me, and my heart instantly clenches even in the state I am in. My throat closes, and my head face plants the kitchen table.

I get a whiff of strong coffee. Mm, it smells good. "Here, drink this." Dana's soft voice filters into my brain as she shoves the cup under my nose. "Did I fall asleep?" I ask groggily. "Sorry, babe." "Yeah. You were out for a few minutes. It's all good, honey. Drink that, and it will make you feel better." The coffee tastes like heaven as I sip it slowly. I drink it until I'm feeling a little more sober, and the more sober I become, the more stupid I feel for getting in such a state. I'm grateful when Logan picks us up in the car and drops everyone off at home. My bed is definitely calling my name.

"Oh my God," I groan.
I roll over in the bed, burying my face in the pillow to shut out the light, moaning because my head feels like someone hit me with a hammer. Jesus, I feel like I drank the bar dry last night. Throwing back the covers and dragging myself out of bed, I head for the shower. I have to work today, and I'm so glad Annie is staying over at her friends until I finish; it means I don't have to worry about rushing her over to the child-minders.
Once I arrive at work, I notice that everything is in its place. It has been obsessively organised. Melissa is already here rushing around, making my head spin. She's all over the place, like a mini- whirlwind, running backward and forward while I watch trying to shake off my headache. I pitch in where I can, working in silence. It gets busy for a while until lunch time when I step out into the street filling my lungs with the warm air; I need coffee and a bacon roll. I make my way up the high street to the place that makes the best hangover bacon butties.

I can feel it in the air. All the hairs stand up on end at the back of my neck. That familiar chill runs up and down my spine. I am being watched; I know I am. I hadn't noticed the unsettling feeling before because I've been too hungover, but I'm definitely feeling it now. It's unnerving. I feel sick to my stomach, and I feel like I am going to have a panic attack right here in the street. I hurry up the road as fast as I can carrying Melissa's and my lunch and drinks. I slip back through the door trying to get control over my breathing. In and out—one, two, three. I count and repeat until my nerves are calm, and my body stops shaking.

"You OK? You look pale. Too many shots last night?" I give her a shaky smile, grasping at my control.

"Yeah. Something like that." I walk behind the counter and hand Melissa her lunch. She smiles and thanks me. A shudder passes through my body. I'm still so on edge, the sick feeling still present in my stomach. Melissa's eyebrows furrow as she watches me sit down at one of the tables.

Lee walks in through the shop door and relief fills me up from the inside. I let out a huge sigh. "Hey, how are you?" I ask.

"Are you feeling better this morning, Rose? Or are you feeling a bit worse for wear?" He gives me that knowing grin that I have the hangover from hell with a concerned look on his face.

"I know; I was in a right state. I'm sorry we all crashed in on you like that," I say shyly, my face heating me up from the inside. I want the ground to swallow me up whole.

"Hey, it's all good. You can come crash in on me anytime you want, no matter what state you get into as long as I know you're OK, and you are safe. That's all that matters to me." He smiles.

"What brings you in here today? Would you like coffee? We have all kinds…"

He cuts me off. "Just a regular coffee please, baby, and I came to see you, of course." He smiles which lights up his whole face. I mirror his smile. As I walk away, I can feel his eyes burning into my back. Behind the counter, I make Lee his coffee and make myself another cup. I feel so much safer having him around I try and think of a way to keep him here longer when I turn and see him sitting in the seat watching me.

Melissa has pulled a chair so close to Lee she may as well be sitting in his lap. The jealousy I feel pulsing through my veins makes my blood boil and bubble up, pissing me off no end for feeling this way. I try and pretend I haven't noticed her paws all over him, but he's clearly feeling uncomfortable—it's written all over his face. I want to shred her eyes out with my claws and feed them to her with a spoon. I carry the coffees over to the table and plaster a fake smile on my face.

As I take my seat next to them, Logan and Dana walk through the door. Dana instantly notices the expression that must be written all over my face as soon as she sees me. "Melissa, can Logan and I get two cappuccinos, please?"

Ha. That shifts her ass away from Lee. He reaches forward, gently sweeping his thumb across my bottom lip. "Rose, is that coffee good? It looks so good on your lips. Would love to lick it off," he whispers. I push my body forward, sliding my hands up his chest. "You would taste so good right now." He closes his eyes, moving his fingers over my jaw, down my neck to my shoulders. The tips of his fingers discreetly brush over the side of my breast. He kisses me on the lips.

"Get a room, you two." Dana is smiling at us like it's the best thing she's ever seen.

It seems to go against every instinct I've got to pull away from him first, because once I stop looking at him and feeling his warmth I don't want to imagine him not being there. Only now do I appreciate how hot he looks today. The narrow dip of his waist, the wide chest underneath a white t- shirt, biceps threatening to break out at the sleeves. I lick my lips when my eyes rake over his throat. I feel the need to suck on his neck and his chest. His jeans are worn and perfectly him. I can imagine the feel of his hands weaving through my hair as I remove his boxer briefs, pushing them down his hips. I swallow back a lump in my throat as it registers in my mind that I can't touch him like I want to in front of everyone here. It takes me a while to pull my eyes away from him, but I do. Reluctantly.

The door of the shop opens and in walks Dembie. I glance over and ask what she would like when I already know the answer but always ask her anyway.

"The usual please, beautiful." She comes in every day, two sometimes three times, for her vanilla latte. She never buys anything other than, but she does use our computers to send out emails and spreadsheets for her shop. With that, Declan walks in and starts getting into a deep conversation with his brother Logan about the football. Men and their balls! I narrow my eyes when they land on Lee's scowling face.

"What?" I ask.

"Stop drooling over your customers." What the hell? I turn away from him, rolling my eyes and scoffing. He's such a dick sometimes. I feel his arms slip around my waist when he whispers in my ear, "You're mine, always will be. Don't you forget that, Rose." He's jealous.

"Wow, am I really?" I question and remove myself from his hold making my way back behind the counter. I need to get back to work, and he needs to leave. I really do not want him to go and leave me here feeling so unsafe without him, but I know he can't stay here with me all day. Once Logan and Declan leave I will be feeling even more unsafe.

Lee shouts over to me, "Baby, I will pick you up when you are finished here then go get Annie. We can do something together." Before I have a chance to say anything, he bids everyone farewell and

then he's gone. I feel the familiar ache in my heart at his loss.

Dembie comes behind the counter when her phone starts going crazy inside her handbag. "Shit, babe, I better take this." She answers the call, scowling at it as she does and walks into the ladies for some privacy. When she returns, she's smiling.

"Hey, what's up? Are you ok?" I ask as I sit down beside everyone at the table.

"All good." She smiles. "How do you ladies fancy a night out in Newcastle at the weekend? It's my friends Hen night, and she's having a Halloween theme, so we get to dress up. It will be awesome! We can get a hotel in Newcastle for the night and go shopping at the Metro Centre the following day. We can do lunch and have a good laugh. What do you think?"

All the girls' eyes are now on me; the expectation clear on their faces at us all going for another girlie night. Even though we just had one not too long ago, we always could have another one, so I relent. Not that it takes much persuading; I'm all for a good night out with my girls.

"OK, let's do it. I'll go and Google hotels, find out where we can book for the night. Two minutes, I'll grab the iPad." Once I'm back in my seat with a fresh cup of coffee I Google hotels; there are hundreds of them. I want something nice but not too expensive with breakfast included. The rest of the girls search on their phones looking for the same thing. Dembie is sitting at one of our computers. Logan and Declan have gone outside to look at Logan's car engine leaving us girls to it. Ryan has joined us and is currently annoying the hell out of Dembie when he's meant to be helping the guys outside. He's funny, though, with that thick Irish accent, but Dembie is trying her best to ignore him. I can see her cheeks pinking, my own face heated for her. Ryan is flirting with her so hard it's almost painful to watch.

Twenty-Five

Lee

The emotion that grips hold of me as I sprint out of the café to my car can only be described as a pure panic. I can't believe what's happening. I don't panic. Lee Young does not panic. I can get a little anxious, but I definitely don't panic. I have learnt to stay in control. But being with her in that tiny room—her smell, her skin—makes my self-control evaporate. I'm unravelling. She has a hold on me unlike any other woman. It's nothing I have experienced before her.

In the relative safety of my home, I collapse on the sofa. I grip the arm tightly willing my hard cock to subside. I had to get away from her. I told her I would be back later to pick her up, but walking in there to find her chatting and laughing but deep in thought was enough to make me hard again. I made a point of reminding her that I will not take no for an answer, but as with everything Rose, every argument or non-argument she throws back in my face, so I didn't give her the opportunity to answer me.

I jump slightly as I hear a loud bang coming from my kitchen followed by another. As I stand to move around the sofa, I pull out my gun from the back of my jeans making my way through to see what the hell is up. Opening the kitchen door, I point my gun at the person making such a noise finding my sister slamming about. Lowering my gun, I fold my arms across my chest and lean against the wall. The sight of my sister so damn angry diminishes the problem in my boxer shorts instantly.
"What the fuck are you doing in here, Katerina?" She looks up at me as if I have no right to be in my own kitchen.
"What? I can't find a goddamn thing in this house. Why do you insist on moving things, Lee?"
I think she has finally lost the plot. I have no idea what she's talking about. "It would help a great deal if you told me what you're looking for."
Wrong thing to say. Shit, her face is so red I can see steam shooting from her ears.
"Are you crazy? Stop moving shit around, Lee." Her eyes narrow on me, her hands firmly on her hips.
"Fucking hell."
"Lee!" my dad calls out. Saved by my father, thank fuck, as she was about to scratch my fucking eyes out by the looks of things.

"Great work in there, by the way. I just spoke to your Uncle Mark, and he couldn't praise you enough and..." He stops and stares wide-eyed at my sister who has started to throw things around the room. A plate just misses my head and smashed into a million pieces.

"Katerina, pull yourself together, girl, you just missed your brother's head," he shouts.

She slams down the plate she was ready to launch at my head again. She straightens, nodding her head, but not before glaring at me again. She grabs her handbag and storms out, slamming every door in the house on her way out of the front door. *What the fuck is her problem?*

My father sits down at the kitchen table looking at me with fire in his gaze. "What have I done?"

"What the hell was all that about? It wouldn't kill you to be a little nicer to your sister, you know."

"Dad, I swear I came in here because I could hear her banging around like some crazed lunatic.

Then she starts launching stuff at my head because she can't find something." He leans forward with a glare, cutting me off.

"Well done, son." He's talking about our last job I presume. We got the diamonds back. We don't have to do another job again. Smithy is out of the woods—he's still in hospital and hating every

second apart from the fit nurses looking after him, but he should be able to go home by the end of the week. I've asked him to come and stay with me until he's fighting fit again."

"How's Uncle Mark doing now, Dad?" My Uncle Mark broke his leg on the job, unfortunately. He was up on the roof at the time, slipped, and landed on his feet, but the fall managed to break three bones in his leg.

"He's home now, son. He's doing OK, but make sure you visit him soon." He cocks his head at me, and I acknowledge the friendly command.

"Dinner at mine tonight, don't be late. It's a two-hour drive, son. No excuses." He stands and makes his way to the door.

"See you there."

Finally, I'm alone, I step back into the living room and collapse on my sofa. OK, I'm a bit on edge. As hard as I try, I just can't seem to focus on a damn thing. Even after being away from Rose a good few hours, by four o'clock I know I have to get out of here, get to my dad's for dinner, then after, pick up Rose and Annie and take them out to the cinema.

Pulling up at my dad's driveway I feel some of the tension slip away. I am immediately engulfed by the familiar smell of my dad's cooking and the chatting of family coming from the kitchen. I step into the room and bend down to kiss my sister on the cheek.

"In a better mood now, I see?" It is more of a question. I need to know if I have to dodge something flying at my head.

"Yes, sorry about earlier I just hate it when I can't find anything. That house is so big it's like searching for a needle in a haystack," she complained.

"Hey, no worries. What's cooking, Dad? It smells delicious," I ask.

"A bit of everything tonight, son. Jamaican," he answers. My dad is an amazing cook. I grab a plate and start digging into the food already set out on the dining room table.

"Lee, I've been meaning to ask you…." my dad begins, handing me a can of beer.

"Would you invite Rose and the little one over to dinner next week, and convince her it's a good idea?" I groan in response and receive a glare followed by a slap across the side of my face from my sister.

"Fuck. OK, I will ask her, but I'm not going to force her to come here," I say rubbing my cheek that is now throbbing from my sister's palm. I glare daggers at her.

"Don't act like a little boy, little brother, and I won't treat you like one." Fucking hell! *What am I, four fucking years old?*

"Hit me again, Katerina, and I'll show you how much of a man I am when I shove my gun—" I don't get to finish the sentence.

"Lee, please can we for once have a nice family meal without you two ripping each other to shreds?" My dad's on his feet. Katerina and I take a seat as he is now shouting. I shut my mouth, and so does the fucking point-scoring bitch. I hate these fucking dinners. No fucking way am I bringing Rose and Annie 'round here next week. It's like walking into World War III.

I get out of there as soon as I finish eating. I know my dad will be pissed, but I will handle that later. I need to leave, go home, and do a workout before I go completely insane. Once I'm home, I lock myself in, needing to expel some of that pent up energy. I increase the speed on the treadmill in the hopes that it distracts me from the shitstorm fucking with my mind. Rose is going on a girlie night, all night. All I want to do is go and kidnap her and lock her in my bedroom until the rest of the girls return. I push myself hard, my feet pounding as my muscles ache. And my chest burns. No matter how hard I try, it fails to distract me from her. From anything. I close my eyes when the treadmill stops, and she's there inside my head. She never leaves, and my dick is rock fucking hard all the time

thinking of her. It's torture. The hunger I feel… I'm consumed by the need for more of those moments with her. I'd do anything she asked me to. It was happening more when I wasn't even with her, what the actual fuck? The sweat drips from every pore in my body. I'm here, but not where I belong. I'm consumed by the dark, the monster deep within me I fight it every fucking day. I'm awake in my own nightmare. I risk my own freedom, shrinking my soul while I am in the lifestyle—it's all I know. I still exist. I'm still alive and breathing. I need to get the fuck out of here and go find her before she leaves.

Dawn A Keane

TWENTY-SIX

Rose

Without conscious, thought my hand travels down to my clit, my fingers circle as I close my eyes and remember last night with Lee. His voice is whispering softly into my ear while his hands roam across my body. *"Tomorrow you will be sore from where I have been, baby. I will make sure you will think about me all the time we are apart from one another, all the time you're away from me."* I come undone right here in my bed, gasping as I recall Lee fucking the life out of me, making me come all over again. I sigh as I roll over. I have to get up. I dig my face into my pillow as far as it will go. I really don't want to, but I need to get organised and take Annie over to stay with Logan's mum and dad at their house. They sometimes take Annie when they look after their own grandchildren. Annie loves it so much because she gets to spend some time with Kayleigh, Amy, and little Jayden. However, this time I get to spend the night in Newcastle on a Hen do with my girls—it's going to be epic. I have spent so long trying to come up with a good fancy dress outfit, and in the end I went with a sexy red devil. The dress is a little short.

There's a hair band that comes complete with horns. I feel a little spark of excitement, and it spurs me into getting my ass moving.

The great thing about Newcastle is it's not that far away from Jedburgh. It's the closest city; we can make it in an hour in the car. Dembie takes us in her car to the hotel. In the end, we booked our rooms at the Premier Inn, The Quayside, with breakfast included. I require a decent full English breakfast after a girlie night out since hangovers hate me so much. I also require plenty of coffee and paracetamol. Just thinking about it is making my mouth water. I can eat that at any time, but having someone else cook for you makes all the difference.

"Dembie! Jesus Christ, slow down, woman." Race car driver was boyfriend number one, and he taught Dembie to drive. She's an awesome driver, but I'm hanging onto my seat. He turned out to be a married man, such a shame for her.

"You're safe with me. Don't worry, dude," Dembie tells me, smirking.

"I know, but could you just maybe slow down a little? I kind of like my face the way it is, babe," I say.

Dembie full on laughs at me while she swerves around the next bend. "We're here, ladies," she squeals in excitement.

Boyfriend number two was a hacker, and he is currently serving a sentence at her majesties pleasure, so she is completely off men at the moment. And I mean, who can blame her? I thought my luck was bad.

Inside our hotel room, I start putting away my stuff then head into the shower while Dana is talking on the phone with Logan and the little ones.

The warm water falls all around my head and down my back when Lee fills my mind. That seductive grin of his makes me sigh while I remember his hands all over my body. Lathering the soap over my breasts without realizing it, my hand travels to my nipple absently twisting it. The touch of my hand feels like his touch in my mind. If I just close my eyes, I can feel his long fingers ghosting along the underside of my breast, his thumbs brushing over my nipples, cupping me with his large hands. I sigh into the warm spray as it washes away the shower gel from my body. Gathering some sensibility, I quickly wash and condition my hair. I must get myself ready. I intend to get smashed tonight; a good blowout and a laugh with the girls will make me forget the bad things that are

happening. Just what the doctor ordered.

There's a knock on our hotel room door.

"Rose, Dana, you two ready? Wow, look at you."

It's her again—Melissa. I don't know what it is with this woman, but there's something about her, and I am not talking about the zombie costume she's currently wearing. I just feel this vibe. She comes across as lovely, but the obsession she has with Lee is unsettling me. Or maybe it's all just in my head since I have been under a lot of pressure recently. I'm just a jealous bitch, my insecurities acting up.

I'm still wrapped in my towel as she follows me into my hotel room. Dembie follows her in running for the toilet. I start to dry my hair with the towel that's wrapped around it when Dembie comes up behind me taking the towel and starts rubbing my head with it.

Too shocked to do anything but stare at her in the mirror, she tells me, "You have such beautiful hair, so curly, and you smell delicious." Well shit! I just stare wide-eyed at her some more while she keeps on talking to me. In that instance, my towel chooses that very moment to drop around my ankles. She puts her hands on my shoulders using her fingers to draw circles along my skin. I can't move— I'm actually frozen to the spot and speechless. I have never in my life looked at another woman in that way before, you know in a sexual way. I don't, but she looks so beautiful. Her reflection gazing back at me... she looks sexy as hell in a scary attractive sort of way in her full face paint and costume. She continues to draw circles over my skin sending tingles right over my whole body; my eyes close without me realising it the moment I feel her fingers slide over my stomach then my eyes snap open.

"What are you doing?" I snap, snatching up my towel from the floor.

"I just appreciate your beauty that's all." She shrugs her shoulders, turns, and answers the loud knocking I'm only just noticing.

Surviving You

Tony is a good friend; he works alongside Dembie. He looks like a Greek God, is as gay as they come, but a great friend. I realise it's him at the door, so I double my efforts and get myself ready. Party time!

A taxi is waiting outside just as we make it down to the entrance doors. "Ready to go, Rose?" Dana says, smiling wide. Her smile so infectious. "I'm as ready as I'll ever be. chick."

We pull up to the kerb of the club Storm and walk into the line that's halfway down the street. It soon goes down, and we head inside after being patted down and searched by the doormen. The music's blasting, and the club is packed. Perfect. Dembie orders our drinks at the bar while the rest of us find ourselves a seat. We have a huge table, and it isn't long before it's filled up with Dembie's friends. Pink feather boas, banners and heels, penis and lip-shaped handbags fill the space. It's like a Freddy Kruger movie at an Ann Summers party. It doesn't take long before Melissa is up on the dance floor grinding on a random guy's leg. Dembie soon drags me up onto the dance floor as Pharrell Williams' "Happy" blasts around us. Tony has got some moves. He dances around us while we watch him in inspiration. Dembie takes my hands as we dance. We laugh and jest until our feet hurt. I leave Dembie to it and make my way over the bar, squinting my eyes closed as I take a seat on the bar stool. Killer heels and dancing do not mix.

"What can I get you, love?"

Giving her my best smile, I lean forward. "Jack and Coke, please, and four blue Wkds." She doesn't give me an answer, just gets on with my order. She then disappears to the other end of the bar to serve the crowd waiting. The rest of the night becomes a blur the more the alcohol is consumed.

I sigh dramatically when I check my mobile phone, a missed call from Lee. I have no idea why he is calling me so damn late. I've been gone a day. He knows I'm spending the weekend with the girls. I put off calling him back. My head hurts and is spinning. I make certain to swallow two painkillers with a large glass of water before I climb into my bed. I'm looking forward to breakfast—that will fix everything.

The aroma of bacon creates a deep rumble. My tummy thinks my throat's been cut the way it keeps growling at me which in turn makes me roll over in the bed. I lie here, curled into the covers on my side, I can hear the sound of someone breathing, and I can feel an arm move over my side, a large hand splayed over my arm, the scent of Lee filling my nostrils. Lee? Lee is here in bed with me. Shock rips through me. I stay completely still. Wonder is filling my mind. Holy shit. Lee is here. But why?

I turn toward him, looking into his eyes. "What the hell are you doing here, Lee? When did you get here?"

He looks at me blankly like I just asked the most stupid thing ever and replied, "I came to see my girl." *His girl? Am I his girl?*

"Lee, you're in my bed." I state the obvious, and he grins at me which annoys me further.

"Yeah, I am." I watch his hand move to his jaw, his index finger rubbing over his lips and his thumb under his chin while he studies me for what feels like a long time. "I'm yours, and you're mine. Our souls are connected, stop fighting it. Stop fighting the inevitable. And stop fighting me." He drags his hand through his hair then cups my cheek; he hasn't finished talking. "Just let me love you, let me in, babe. Please don't keep pushing me away because I won't let you do it. I'm not going anywhere. No matter how hard you push."

I remain silent because, honestly, I am a little lost for words and afraid my alcoholic morning breath will knock him out. *Ugh.* He sighs deeply.

"I'm not a knight in shining fucking armour, baby, I never have been. My heart is black and cold; some say it's made of stone. But I worship the ground you walk on. You're thawing out a part of my heart I thought I had lost forever."

Tears start to form in my eyes, but I hold them back and lunge forward kissing him. Fuck the morning breath. I twist my body around his, the cover still between us. My hands are in his hair tugging at it gently, his soft curls tickling my palms as I do. His own hands slide through my hair as he deepens the kiss, his tongue sparring with mine.

He pulls away. "How long can I have you like this?" he asks and proceeds to trail feather-light kisses along the skin at my neck, his lips so warm and soft.

"We have to talk," I breathe through each soft kiss.

"No talking, not now. Later." I swallow and take a few breaths to collect my thoughts. *What am I doing? Wait how did he get in here?* I roll off the bed and stand looking down at him, hand on hips.

"Stop. Who let you in here? This is supposed to be a girls' weekend. You know, females only, spending time together. I don't see your vagina, Lee."

He suddenly stops dead and grins at me. "What do you see, baby?"

"At this moment in time all I see is a big dick, that big dick being you." He rolls on his back and starts laughing, full on laughing at me, while he clutches his obvious erection in his hand.

"This, dick, baby?" He looks beautiful. I have to stare at him; I can't not stare at him, especially as he fists his cock in front of me. My anger at him suddenly melts away. He rolls off the bed so fast I nearly miss it. He pulls me back down with him. I land on my back with his hard body pressed on top of me, his hard on pointed in all the right places.

"You're so bad, Lee." I stare up into his eyes, smiling.
"I'm as bad as they come. I'll be as bad as you want me to be. I would walk in front of a bullet for you and your girl. You love me, though. I can feel it." He pauses and stoops down to drag his lips across mine. "I'm also hungry. I think I'll just have you for breakfast." His eyes bore into mine, his mouth moving over mine again as he kisses me with more purpose, his intention clear.
"You still haven't answered my question. How did you get in here?" I ask, pushing my hands into his chest. He sighs, kisses me on the forehead and places his hands at each side of my head pushing himself up.
"I paid for the room. They said you didn't have to pay your bill until you checked out. I told them I'm your man and I'm here to surprise you, plus I threw in an extra hundred for their trouble." I stare at him blankly for a long, long time. I can feel my own eyes turning round and wide while I try to process what he just said to me and wondering if he actually did just say it.

"You really are so bad, Lee. I can pay my own damn bill. I can't believe they let you do that! You could be a bloody serial killer for all they know," I shriek at him, utterly perplexed.

His hands still at either side of my head, he tilts toward me and plants soft kisses across my cheek and whispers, "But I'm not a serial killer. I don't kill for the fun of it, baby. Anyone ever tries to hurt you or Annie with me around they will have to try damn fucking hard to get through me first."

I come unstuck, wrapping my hands in his soft curls, locking my lips onto his. He rests on one elbow and curls his other hand in my hair, deepening the already frenzied kiss. I can't get enough. His hand starts to move, caressing my breast through my pink slip, hardening my nipple just with one simple touch. His colossal hand moves up and down the satin slip I'm wearing, over my hip and stomach, and back up to my breast. He rolls my nipple between his thumb and finger while our tongues lap at each other.

"Speaking of bullets...." I grin at him, jumping off the bed to my suitcase, retrieving the little bullet I was given at the Hen party, a pink and black one. I press the top, and it starts to vibrate in my hand. Lee is on the bed sitting on his feet with a fiery thirst dancing in his eyes. I rush at him, pushing him back against the mattress, lust filling his eyes when I take the bullet and run it along his balls underneath, my other hand gripping his erection.

"Fuck, yes..." he moans. Slow, feather-light strokes as I run the bullet over where I know it will drive him wild. He groans. Reaching for me, he slides his fingers through my hair gripping the back of my head. I start to run the bullet along his shaft along to the tip, his body shuddering as the sensation rips through his body. His hand moves to my back flipping me over so he's on top of me. Taking the bullet out of my hand, he runs it along my breast then along my tummy in a circular motion. Making me giggle and lift my arms up hitting him in the face.
"Oh, I'm so sorry," I tell him, feeling terrible for nearly taking his eye out, yet laughing all the same.
"How sorry are you, baby? Sorry enough to let me punish you with my dick?" he says with lust-filled eyes and a grin on his lips. He pins my arms above my head, his knees push my legs open as his lips crash down, kissing my neck with force, devouring every inch of skin.
He nips my ear with his teeth, grinding his hips between my legs saying, "Those knickers are damn sexy, but they need to come off." His smile is like the sunshine on a dull day. His eyes are glistening.
I hear the bullet start to vibrate again as he moves down my body, his soft lips trailing gentle kisses as he moves farther down followed by the vibrations. The sensation is hitting me deep down into every nerve ending making my body shudder against his. I'm a goner.

TWENTY-SEVEN
Lee

I close my eyes tight again, pulling Rose toward me for a kiss. "Mmmm, baby," I whisper against her mouth. "I need to be inside you so badly."

She pulls my face in front of hers, cupping my cheeks in her tiny, soft hands, and in that one look I can see just how much I mean to her. Just with one look on her magnificent face. Dipping my head, I press my lips against her neck as she whimpers into my hair. The kiss grows deeper as I crawl on top of her, feeling her warm, soft body underneath mine. I gasp as I start to lose control again, a pained groan slipping from my mouth, my stomach clenching, and my cock solid as stone. As she lies underneath me, I run the bullet over her bud, over the thin material still covering her breasts, her nipples poking through, screaming to get out. I rip her free of it and continue to torture her with the sensation. My hips grind against her hot little pussy as she shudders underneath me.

I remove her black, lace knickers, a possessive groan escaping my lips as I dip my head forward and lick along the seam, pressing the bullet into her clit. I inhale her scent that I love so much. Reaching out, I run my fingertip down her slit. Her hips buck as she closed her eyes, and she lets out a long moan that I feel to the very depths of me. She's soaking wet, dripping on my fingers. My cock is throbbing as I watch where my hand is going, running my lips over the inside of her thigh. Swiping my tongue along her slit. The taste of her filling my mouth in turn makes me start lapping, devouring her. Her hands tug at my hair making me lose it even more.

Pushing her legs wide apart, I run the bullet back over her swollen clit, my finger slipping in and out, my balls aching with the need to fuck her hard. My nostrils flare as I watch her bite at her bottom lip, my heart pounding just looking at her. Rose's legs began to shake, and she digs her nails into my back as she pulls me toward her. Pulling my finger free, I am so fucking hard for her. I need to hear her calling out my name. I need to be inside her now. Bending down, I suck her nipple into my mouth while kneading at the other.

"I need you inside me, Lee," Rose moans. Her hand comes around my cock, and she begins stroking it back and forth which makes me hiss through my teeth, my balls tight while she works me. A growl rumbles from my chest, but I am unable to speak. I have no words. I push her back on the mattress feeling so connected to her it makes my own body shake as I enter her, sliding in deep. A connection I've never felt to any other, souls connected while our bodies are.

"You bring out the good in me, turn the darkness to dust." My voice breaks. "I am yours. My heart is ready to burst. What have you done to me? I love you so hard, Rose. You take me out of the dark. You have shown me the light," I whisper in her ear as she breathes heavily.

"I love you too, Lee." Her breath hitches. "You take away the demons that haunt my dreams, and my fate doesn't seem so bleak." Using all my strength not to squash her small frame and using my thighs to push between her legs, I slide out then back in, her hands touching every inch of my back. I look down at her—my woman, she's mine. The other half of my soul.

Surviving You

I lie watching her as the lights from outside illuminate the room. This marks the beginning of the rest of our lives. She is so beautiful; her soft dark curly hair fanned out over the pillow, her chest rising and falling with each of her breaths. Her soft plump lips make my cock hard while I watch her sleep. I trace my fingers over the two butterfly wings that dance up her hip. Her eyes flicker as I whisper her name to stir her.
"Baby, wake up," I breathe against her lips as I plant gentle kisses over her mouth and along her jaw.
"Lee," she murmurs sleepily, and I smile because she whispered my name.
"Rose, wake up."
Her eyes flicker open, and she smiles, my hard chest against the soft fullness of her breasts. Her hand comes up to rest against my ribcage. I can feel the heat of her against my skin. She skitters her fingers across my pecs and over my sides, her thumbs curving the outline of the muscles on my back so softly I swallow against the sensation. Fuck!
"You were made for me, a dark angel sent from heaven," she whispers into my ear as she plants soft kisses there.

I've had my fair share of women over the years, but not a single one of them ever made me feel like I do right now. Her fingers leave a trail of electricity in their wake, each touch shooting through my veins and into my cock. Her soft lips a heat, making me feel like I have a fire burning through me. Her tongue—tasting—licks and nips at my skin lighting up my already burning body.

"Rose," I breathe as she licks a line all the way down my spine, worshipping me, and the pleasure takes hold. She pulls on the strands of my hair. I let out a growl from inside my throat.

"Can I keep you?" I ask.

My heart beats so fast at the severity of want on her face that my heart just might shatter into a thousand pieces. I squeeze her in my arms so close; I am scared to ever let her go. Scared I will drive her away somehow. Her tongue licks its way along my flesh again, untamed growls ripping from my throat. Then she palms at her breasts, pinching her nipples as she watches me dip my hand down. I begin sliding my cock up and down while I moan.

"Lee, please," she begs one more time, and I can't take any more of the best torture I've ever had. I lurch forward, my hands smoothing up and down her thighs, over her hips, her waist, eventually moving to cup her breasts. I watch her eyes ignite with need. She starts slowly stroking her hand up and down my cock. I am falling apart. Feeling her wetness as I move my cock flush against her pussy, she moans into my mouth, her hand squeezing at my bulging biceps. I flip her around and bend her over, her cheek pressed into the pillow. She whimpers at my touch on her ass cheek. I nudge my cock at her entrance, my thick thighs resting against hers. I push the tip in, teasing a little. Gripping her hips with my hands, I begin pushing forward. I surge into her tight, wet heat, slamming my cock until I am fully rooted.

"Lee," she screams out as I roar, my hands shaking as I reached down, covering her back, my hot breath panting into her hair.

"Shit," I groan, and I rock my hips back and forth, my dick scraping against her g-spot. "Rose, baby."

I grunt as my hand brushes her hair from her back and my lips press against the skin on the nape of her neck, making her shiver. I rumbled out a growl as her channel clenches tight, wrapping around my cock. Growing bigger, I thrust inside her faster, and deeper, wild, and focusing on making us both come. My thighs tighten against her legs as the delicious sensation burns through me. Stilling and bellowing out as I come, she moans, coming right along with me. Her body shakes as the orgasm hits her. Little mewls catch up on whispered breaths as she hits her peak with me. I wrap my arm around her stomach as I gently pull out and pull her back with me so she's straddled in my lap. Lying with my back against the pillow, I hold her tight against me. She's mine and always will be. I will die protecting her. I will not let anyone hurt her again.

"I see the girl in you, standing on a chair in a pink nightgown in the dark. You see me standing against my window. You jumped. I saw you, startled as you wondered what made me cry. My palms are flat against the window pane. The tears are streaming freely down my cheeks like the heavens have opened, like the rain has started to pour down all around me. Stained with blood—the blood I had just spilled as a boy. The big black cloud weighing heavy on my heart." I stop for a minute to gather myself to continue. "But I see you, you never take your eyes away from me as you move in closer, my pain ripping my insides out as the darkness turns out the light. But I see you, I see your light shining so brightly in the dark. As you lean against the cold glass. Your heart breaking as you helplessly watch as my pain burns my heart. You press your hands and small cheek against the glass, your breath steaming up the window. You want to help me; I want you to help me. You do the only thing you can and reach out to me." My breath hitches as I remember. "That small but oh-so- meaningful gesture stops me from falling into the dark pit of hell. I saw you. I always saw you, but I kept away until now. I see you now, Rose. I see you now," I whisper, rubbing my nose gently against hers.

"That was you? You are that boy?" Her eyes grew round and disbelieving, her arms wrapping around my neck as her lips press gently on my own while her salty tears roll down her cheeks and into our mouths.

TWENTY-EIGHT

Rose

The chill from the morning air seeps into my skin. Goosebumps prickle across my arms as I wake from a deep sleep. "Hey, Rose, wake up," a low voice whispers into my ear. I feel his warm body pressed against my back, and the covers have now been removed from me. I tug on Lee's hand and pull it in toward my cleavage in an attempt to keep me warm. I yelp, my eyes flying open in surprise as his warm body leaves me as he walks to the window to close it again. We'd fallen asleep so late. I am cold and tired, and I know I have to move, but I don't want to. I am more than happy staying here all day.

I move my tired legs into the bathroom where he has already filled the bath with water and bubbles. He steps into the bath and grins, pulling me toward him, gently turning me so I am sitting in front of him, my back pressing against his hard muscled chest. We sit in the bath, washing each other. I am beginning to wake up fully. I suck in a breath as his soft, lathered hands sweep across me.

"You have to learn to trust me, Rose," he breathes into my ear, his warm breath ghosting across my neck.

"I know," is all I can manage at the moment. I take a while before speaking again. "I told you that's all I want, to let go of my past. I want nothing more than to put all of my trust in you, Lee. Has anyone ever told you that you're arrogant and maybe in need of anger management?" I breathe deeply, the sensation of his hands rubbing the soap over my breasts taking my breath away.

"You're like my bright shooting star across a dark sky," he says as he starts to stroke rhythmically up and down my spine. My head falls back against his shoulder as he laughs. "Baby, I'm whatever you want me to be, whenever you need me." He finishes rinsing away the soap and slips out of the bath, wrapping a towel around his huge frame. He takes me by the hand and pulls me out toward him, wrapping me in his towel, pressing a gentle kiss to my lips. Somehow we end up back in bed, and Lee shows me just how much he thinks I should put my trust in him until we fall asleep.

I head down to the dining area leaving the sex God on legs fast asleep in bed. I find a table and sit down. White table cloths cover almost everything: seat covers, tablecloths, curtains. The walls are decorated very lightly. Flicking through the menu, I scan it, but I already know what I want. The waitress appears, a tall, thin woman, with her notebook in her hand ready to take my order.

"What would you like this morning?" she asks, no smile or even an ounce of friendliness on her face.

"Full English, and a vanilla latte, please," I say, not really in the mood for her abruptness. Lee sure worked up my appetite this morning, not that I'm complaining. Dana appears, looking amazing in black jeans and a red tank top, no sign of having a hangover. She joins me at my table.

Sitting down, she orders the same as me when the waitress disappears. When she walks away, Dana asks, "What's her fucking problem?"

"No idea, a bad day maybe." I shrug. "How are you feeling this morning? It was a good night last night. I had a surprise visit from Lee in the middle of the night. Although, I didn't see him until I woke up this morning." I chuckle, thinking back to what we've been up to all morning.

"Logan's here too. I thought you looked a bit flushed, sweet cheeks." She giggles.

"Piss off, my god. Tell everyone in here, why don't you, chick?" My face turns beetroot.

"What? That your man made you scream out his name?" Dana laughed.

"And how would you know that, being too busy screaming out Logan's name to notice. Where is

he anyway? Did you tire him out? We had fun with that bullet I got last night."
She placed her hand on my arm gently. "Something like that. He's flat out, babe. My God, I won't be able to look Lee in the eyes again." Her cheeks turn red. I have never seen her get embarrassed before. We both double over laughing like a couple of schoolgirls. I nearly fall out of my seat.
The waitress reappears with our drinks. I sip mine back, the warm liquid sliding down my throat, the taste of coffee and vanilla awakening my taste buds. Delicious. I really need the caffeine fix to cure the horrendous hangover that plagues me. Dana is about to when she drops it, spilling it all over the white tablecloth. Her face has an expression of shock all over it like she has seen a ghost.
"Dana, what's wrong? Are you OK?" She doesn't speak just stared out the window. I follow her train of sight and instantly freeze in my seat. I can't move; I can only stare at the figures across the street staring right back at us. How long have they been standing there? How do they know we are here?
"Rose, let's move." Dana is up on her feet pulling at my arm. I start to shake but am able to run out of the dining area with her.

"I have to go get Lee," I shout without meaning to, pure and utter panic taking over my whole body.
"Calm down, everything's going to be fine, OK? The guys are here. Let's go." We run our separate ways.
I get to the lift, pressing the button. It isn't coming down, so I abandon it. "Fuck."
I run through the door taking the stairs two at a time. Four flights up, I trip and slip down the steps scraping my knee. Pain shoots through my leg. Gripping onto the handrail, I launch myself up pushing myself forward. My heart rate has accelerated, and I'm pretty sure it's going to rip from my chest it's beating so hard. I make it to the right floor running through the door to my hotel room. I stop dead in front of it, fear gripping hold of me and squeezing my heart like a vice. What if he's not there?

TWENTY-NINE

Lee

Bang!

"Wake the fuck up!"

My eyes open ever-so-slightly as the sound of gunshots awaken me, the sound of my childhood rattling around in my brain. I'm dreaming. My dreams are turning into my reality. I don't want to open my eyes the rest of the way. What the actual fuck is happening? Peeling my eyes open fully from tiny slits, I am blinded by the light of some fucker's torch.

Where the fuck am I? Last thing I remember is making my woman scream she came so damn hard. My hand moves of its own accord to the back of my head where it's wet and stings like a bitch. Some fucking bastard hit me. I pull my hand away and see it is covered in blood. Shit. Where's Rose?

Anger builds in my blood as I lie here dazed as fuck trying to see who stands above me. When I get on my feet, I will ram that torch down the fucker's throat. Rage fills me up, spurring me on, making my legs and body move. I need to get on my feet, kill this fucker, and find Rose. It feels like I've been drugged; my limbs are so heavy, and I can barely lift my head. What the hell?

"I'm gonna kill you, motherfucker!" I shout to the figure above me. I can't make out what he's saying in return; his voice sounds like a muffled echo like he's far away. The light from the torch sails toward my face, a sharp pain slicing like a knife through my skull then the darkness consumes me.

I wake up cold and shivering in the dark, my sins evidently catching up with me. I'm going to die without ever seeing her beautiful face again, the only woman I've ever let inside my heart, mind, and soul. I won't let that happen, not before I kill this fucktard. I'll give anything to bury myself balls deep inside her pussy, fucking her hard and slow until she's screaming my name and coming all over my dick again.

"Take that blindfold off this fucker," a man's voice orders. The stupid idiots can't even do that right. I could see perfectly fine if the torch wasn't flashing in my eyes. The man's hands loosen the blindfold removing it, but the torch still blinds the fuck out of me. I can't see shit.

"I'll rip your fucking throat out," I threaten whoever these assholes are.

"You've taken what's mine," says a calm voice. "You're going to pay for that. I don't think you're in much of a position to do anything now, are you, Lee?" The fucking dick laughs in my face, and I swear if I could have moved I'd have rammed that smug looking face of his up his ass already.

"And what might that be that you think belongs to you? You do know you've just fucked with the wrong man." My hands shake behind my back, wrapped inside the restraints they have me in as I fight not to explode with temper. I picture her in my mind; her brown eyes and pale skin, rosy red cheeks. Her long dark wavy hair. All I see is her lying on the floor covered in blood. Dead. Those beautiful eyes vacant and wide. And here I am tied up by a motherfucking retard. I can't save her. Because I'm here, and I can't protect her, it torments my mind.

"What the fuck was that?" one of the men hisses as I am dragged into the centre of the room, my head still spinning from the blows I had taken to my head. I had been taught young to take a beating; I'd always been numb to the pain. I am a fighter, a fighter with a burning desire for revenge.

"Lee!" one of the men snaps. His booming voice makes me freeze. I stared into his eyes moving forward until I stand before him, towering above his frame. I tilt my head to the side, studying the man's face.

"I said you had better hurry up and kill me, because if you wait too long—" I pause for emphasis

"—I will kill you."
His fist makes contact with my jaw; I can taste the blood now dripping into my mouth. I raise my head and spit the blood into the man's face. The fucker snarling in front of me turns my head the other way where there is another man staring at me. His shades are sitting on top of his head look fucking ridiculous with the balaclava covering his face, turning back to the other man with green eyes narrowed on me. His thick-set arms cross his chest. I grunt just as a wave of nausea clouds over my body, and I sway from side to side on the spot. I try to fix my attention forward, seeing this cocky as fuck man talk to the other guy. Vomit is crawling its way up my throat. I stand here, tied up, watching the men speak as my throat closes and I freeze. I need to breathe; I am losing it. I can't take being tied up and kept here against my will, caged like an animal. My body burns with the need to kill. My throat tenses—these men are dead; all I can see is red. My nostrils flare, my hands itching to rip both their fucking heads clean off and watch their blood spill in front of me. My arm muscles strain, but I am unable to move them being tied behind my back.

Their lives will be mine to take once I get free of the restraints. I snap. And roar. And dive at the men. I knock one of them back and lean forward to see the fear in his green eyes. I smile, knowing he's fucking scared. Raising my foot, I send a blow to his stomach while the other guy tries to knock me off my feet. I strike again, my heart pounding with the rush. I growl as I kick his stomach again and manage to knock the other guy on his ass with just my shoulder. I kick the guy on the ground in the face, his blood splattering around his head, roaring as I do. My muscles twitch as I keep the blows coming to his head. I lean down and land another blow to his neck. When the other guy tries to rush me, I send him flying back into the wall, his head cracking off it with the force. *Bring it on,* there's no fucking way I'm dying here today.

THIRTY

Rose

My head is spinning. I puff out short breaths trying hard not to fall flat on my face as Dana and Logan run into the back of me at the doorway and stop dead as they take in the sight in front of us. I don't know how long I have been standing here frozen. I can't think straight. Had someone robbed the room, and Lee had stopped them? Did they get the better of Lee and hurt him? I start to shake and find my legs sprinting across the room to the bed seeing the sheets covered in blood. Had they attacked him in his sleep? I turned, staring wide-eyed at Dana, noticing Logan is on his phone.

"What the hell happened?" A woman, a maid, enters the room.

"We are trying to find out," Logan tells her still with his ear to his phone. "Have you called the police?" she asks sounding panicked.

Logan takes over the situation as he says, "Yeah, I called them. Let's get these ladies downstairs; none of you need to stand in here any longer." He looks down at me with piercing, sea-blue eyes, trying to reassure me. "We'll find him."

My lip begins to tremble, and I feel tears sting my eyes. "Where is he? He was right here. I left him asleep in bed," I ask anyone. Logan puts his arm around my shoulder and his other arm around Dana's waist and walks us out of there.

I finish giving the police my statement and look across the small room we have been holed up in for the past two hours. Logan and Dana are finishing up giving theirs. I need to get out of here.

"What now?" I ask my friends.

"Now, I'm taking you ladies home," he says simply. I follow.

I am scared out of my mind not only for Lee but for Annie and myself as well. I have to get home to my baby and hold her in my arms. Logan has called the guys—he assures me they're all out searching for him, and there's a whole crew from Manchester searching for him as well as his family and the police. But I can't just sit around here doing nothing, feeling afraid and worried out of my overly-troubled mind. I don't even have my car.

Once I get home with Annie, I start calling people. Friends, family—anyone that might know how to track Lee down. I've called the police six times already, and they're not helping. There's nothing I can do but pace my living room floor and wait. I'm a sitting duck. Mike is out there somewhere with Ian, Dana's ex-husband. How on earth those two met is beyond me. However, that doesn't matter. What matters is that I do not let him near us.

Annie's had her dinner and bath by the time we get home. She's in her nightgown, and I decide the best course of action would be to get into the office at the café. I can't just sit here doing nothing. I call a taxi and drop Annie off with Dana for the night and head in. Logan insists on sending one of the guys over to keep an eye on me; he won't let me go alone, says it isn't safe. He is behind me in his car all the way to the cafe and parked outside across the street sitting there in his car. I do feel a lot safer, but there is no need for him to sit there for however long it takes me to make my calls and do some work. When I arrive at the café all the lights are still on; Melissa must still be working. Just what I don't need right now.
"Oh, hey, I didn't think you would be back in so soon what with everything going on," Melissa says, looking up at me from her desk and closing her laptop.
"I need to keep busy, try and help. You can go; I'll finish up here."
"I really don't mind working on. I still have things to finish up here. Jane called earlier to check in

with you; she said everything's going great. I can help you, if you like?" Oh, Jane, well that's some good news, I suppose.

"That's great, I'm so glad she's doing OK. I have been meaning to call her, but I'll do it later. And thank you for being here, but I just want to be on my own and keep busy you know. No offence." Melissa smiles and relents. Switching off her laptop and grabbing her belongings, she disappears, leaving me alone with my very bleak thoughts.

THIRTY-ONE

Mike

"Ian, what the fuck are you doing here?"

I look down on my new brother standing at my front door. He starts to walk toward me, his hair scraped back in a ponytail, a frown firmly fixed on his face. I move aside to let him in and close the door behind him.

Once inside the dim-lit apartment, I look across and snap at him. "What the fuck? I'll ask you again—What you are doing here?" My hands are out in front of me, palms facing upwards. I'm getting impatient waiting for him to speak to me. Ian's hand suddenly lands on my shoulder, and I turn my head to look where his hand is. He keeps it there as the frown on his face deepens further, as though he's afraid to speak.

"I want to know what it is you're planning to do. We can't keep that motherfucker locked up in there for much longer. You need to end him before others come looking for him." He pauses mid- sentence as if thinking. "And they will, they are probably out there searching for him already. You know who he is, Mike."

"I'm well aware of what I need to do. For now, I'm enjoying playing with him."

Ian nods his head in understanding. He takes his arm from my shoulder and moves to sit down on the chair at the small table in the kitchen. "You need to focus on the job. I get that he's been fucking your wife, taken what belongs to you, but if you do not kill him soon, I fucking will."

I run a hand down my face, my stomach rolling. My hand moves on its own at lightning speed, gripping tightly around his throat. His hands wrap around my wrist as he struggles to suck in the air. I can feel my fingers crushing his windpipe. "Don't tell me what I need to do!" I spit at him. "You aren't in a position to tell me how I should do things, my friend." My gaze is fixed on him; his eyes are wide with fear, his face a deep shade of red.

"I know what needs to be done, Ian. I've been constantly working to make sure our wives come back to us, and I'll make damn sure they do. I'll make it so there is nobody left to help them, nowhere left to run. I'll make sure that they see the error of their whore ways, you get me?" I squeeze on his neck a little tighter. "When that day comes, Rose will relent. She's weak as fuck, and she will have no choice but to come back to me. She'll never leave me again. Like my father had done before me with my mother, a wife must know her place; she must always obey her husband. Rose will be punished accordingly then she will go back to being a good wife or she will die."

Ian has turned a nice shade of blue while making strangled choking noises. I remove my hand from his throat and pull him up to his feet. Patting him on the arm, I ask, "Whisky? Let's celebrate. "

Ian soon passes out on the sofa oblivious to the bitch that has arrived. I stare down at the ugly, tragic-looking excuse of a woman that stands trembling in front of me. Bright red blood trickles down her face from her nose from where I just pounded her face with my fists. Stupid fucking whore trying to plan a night out on her own without me to meet her. Stupid bitch whore mates! I don't fucking think so. Does she really think that I would allow it so she could fuck some other poor bastard? Sink her claws into another unsuspecting chump? Not fucking likely.

I grab her by her arm and pull her toward me. My fist connects with her cheek bone making that cracking sound that turns me the fuck on and makes my cock so fucking hard. Leaning my head down towards the blood exploding from her cheek I slip my tongue out and lick up toward the now colouring wound. Closing my eyes, I savour the taste in my mouth while she whimpers.

"What the fuck have I told you about making plans and not asking me if it's OK first?" I snap at her, boring my eyes into her bright-green, tear-filled ones. She parts her lips as if to speak but quickly closes them again. "I asked you a fucking question, bitch, and I expect you to answer it." She cowers and starts to sob against me some more. I need to fuck the sense back into her brain before I explode inside my fucking boxers.

"Get your clothes off. I need to fuck." She jumps and starts to strip—good girl. "See it's easy just do as I ask. Do you understand, Lola?" Her bra comes off exposing her big, fake, perky tits, and my hand reaches out for them automatically.

"Yes, I'm so sorry I should have run it by you first, I promise I won't do it again." I bite down on her nipple making her sob louder then she lets out a moan like she enjoyed it.

I push her down to her knees. "That's right." Freeing my rock-hard cock from my jeans and swiping it over her lips, I demand, "Suck." Her lips wrap around the tip of my cock as my hand grips the back of her hair tight, and I push her head forward and fuck her mouth. Her green eyes are looking up at me grow wide while I thrust in and out with force. She hangs onto my thighs as if trying to hold herself up as I assault her mouth. I pull out my cock. Still holding her by her hair, I lean down to her level, pushing her down into the floor on her back. I use my other hand and brutally push three fingers into her pussy. She gasps. I place my mouth around her clit and bite down making her buck her hips as I push a fourth finger inside her and fuck her hard with my hand. It's not enough, I need more, I need to be ramming my cock inside her. Flipping her onto her stomach while she gasps for air to fill her lungs I slam my hard cock into her, pushing her body into the cold hard floor.

"Hands against the wall," I bark out the order, and she quickly does as she's told. I ram my stiff cock into her pussy and fuck her until she bleeds and cries and hurts, all the time thinking about my Rose. I want nothing more than to bury my cock in her tight little pussy and make her scream for mercy.

I will have her again when I get rid of her pathetic friends. One down, a dozen more or so to go. I will not let them get in my way and try and stop me. She's mine, and she fucking belongs to me. I have extra help in the form of people just like me. What a stroke of fucking luck it was meeting Ian in my local club. He's a sadistic bastard and wants the same as I do; his wife back where she belongs. We soon realized our wives were together and started tracking them. Ian had already found a lead to his mate's ex-wife's phone in Newcastle. We lost them again, but it was only a matter of time before we found out where they were hiding. After that, it was easy. I will kill them all if I need to—no skin off my nose—but I will teach her a fucking lesson she'll never forget. And soon.

Thirty-Two

Ryan

This morning I wake up in the pub. I still have my pint held firmly in my right hand I haven't spilt a drop of it. Some of the blokes and I had gotten together for a game of poker and drank the night away. I still hadn't heard anything about my boys, and I couldn't stand just to sit around doing nothing, so I ended up in here. Got drunk, played poker, passed out.

We played cards into the early hours of the morning. Nine pints later, I get lucky. Very fucking lucky.

Smithy takes another drag of his cigarette, inhaling the smoke deep into his lungs and blows it back out through his nose.

"That shit will kill you, mate." I grin, placing down the unfinished, unspoiled pint still glued to my palm on the table.

"Mate, I'm still fucking breathing; it will take a lot more than that to finish this pretty face off," Smithy says, squashing his cigarette into the ashtray full of ends on the table.

I laugh, but I feel so fucking grateful that he's still here fully recovered from the coma he had been in for weeks. He looks good; he has some colour back in his cheeks, a spring back in his step and he's even started to put some weight back on. "Grand to have you back with us, my friend," I say, placing my cards on the table looking Dave straight in the eyes. A knowing, cocky-as-fuck grin crosses my lips as he stares down at my winning hand.

"What the hell, you lucky Irish bastard." His hand swipes over his face and hair. He hands over the huge wad of cash and the keys to the run down old gym at the back of Queen Street. I stand and take his hand in mine for a handshake.

"It's been a real pleasure doing business with you, my friend." I smile at Smithy giving him a chin lift before walking out of the pub doors with the biggest smile on my face and a spring in my step. Now I've just got to track down the whereabouts of Lee and Sniper and get their asses back home where they belong.

I find my car where I had abandoned it after a twenty-five-minute search, convinced that some tosser had moved it on me. I drive to McDonald's for some breakfast. After going through the drive- through, I park the car in the car park so I can fill my empty stomach and make some calls.

"Motherfucking Eejit, what does Lee fucking hire you for? Get your fat ass back on it, and help me find my brother." Way pissed off, I scream at Lee's lawyer, breaking the screen on my phone. My intention was to kill the call not my fecking shite phone, which now has a blank cracked screen.

"Fuck," I hiss through gritted teeth as I glare at it, my mind racing with all kinds of thoughts. It has been since I got the call that Lee had been taken. Those eejits better run 'because if I get my hands on them I'll make them wish they were already dead. I then get the call: we got a lock on Sniper.

I am making my way up to the middle of feck knows where to take his furry ass home. I reach the bottom of a hill covered in trees. Looking up I see there's a cliff face with a fucking castle hiding behind those tall trees. I pull the car up on the grass verge as close as I can to the bottom of the cliff. It's a grand view during the day, but it's pitch black right now. How the fuck did the Scots manage way back when without a fecking torch, technology, or even a damn car? I search inside the glove box for my torch, my knife, and some of Sniper's favourite gravy bone biscuits. He loves those things. I was going to bring him a bone, but he wouldn't want to move until he had chomped his way through it all. I'd be waiting all bastard night, so instead I brought his treats. I've left the bone in Lee's where

I've semi-moved in. He seems to like having me around. Beats rattling around on my own in my flat.
I have known Lee for a long time. I've lost count how many years we have spent getting into all kinds of trouble together—he always has my back, I'll always have his, so long as I'm still breathing air into my lungs. The bloke saved me from my messed up life. From my own mind.
I pull out my phone, forgetting that it's cracked to shit. Lee's dad is meant to be meeting me here, and just as I slide it out of my jeans pocket, I see car lights up ahead. Right on time. I rake my fingers through my hair. Then Lee's dad voices what I am thinking. "What fucking sort of place is this to keep a dog in. He definitely here?"
I shrug my shoulders at him. "Just got here, old man, but I fucking hope so," I say. "I'll fucking kill the cunts if he's hurt," he tells me.
"I will kill them even if he's not," I promise him and nod in silent agreement.
Marcus pulls out his phone. "I want every fucking person tied to this to be grilled. Someone knows where my son is, do your job and coordinate," he growls into the phone.
I take direction from Marcus, and we start the climb the steep as fuck stone steps slippery by the mud that cover them. I slip for a third time down the motherfucking medieval steps—bloody evil, all right. Marcus just continues to glare at me like I've just grown a new testicle.

"You're not right in the head, Ryan. You know that, right?" I grin, pissing him off further. He continues to curse at me under his breath as we climb our way up the stupidly steep cliff face. The thunder starts to roll above our heads, the wind whipping against the tall trees all around us. "This place better not be haunted, Ryan, and how the fuck do know he is in here?" he asks.

"Tracker in his chip. Lee had it fitted just in case it was ever stolen. It took a while to track him down being all the way out here in the middle of nowhere," I say, pointing toward the tall, old castle with an iron gate at the top of the cliff. I shine the torch around checking to see where the edges are, where they start and where they end. I point it toward Marcus's face.

"Stop fucking around," he curses, and I chuckle, shining my torch on the old iron gate. "You sure he's in there?" Marcus asks.

Breaking the lock off the gate with my bolt cutters, the chain crashing to the ground, I say, "Only one way to find out." The old iron gate starts to creak as it opens on its own. Marcus and I look at each other feeling way freaked the fuck out. Quickly, I swing the gate back the rest of the way and we walk inside. "Fuck me, it's like something out of that paranormal shit on TV," I say out loud.

Marcus punches me in the arm. "Shut the fuck up."

The enclosed walls are dark, covered in moss. As I shine my torch over them, a mist of anger rips through my body. "Fuckers keeping him locked away in here." I storm forward making my way along the narrow halls of the castle.

"Fatlips Castle is a Pele tower situated at the top of Minto crags, above the river Teviot. It was built in the sixteenth century by the notorious Border Reivers. Its twenty-six feet nine inches from the north to the south, and thirty-two feet three inches from the east to the west. Four storeys inside plus an attic. The Border Reivers were raiders along the Anglo-Scottish border, their ranks consisted of both Scottish and English families and by all accounts they raided the entire border country."

Marcus stopped dead. He stared at me for a long time, so I stopped next to him, wondering what the fuck he was staring at. "What?" I say.

"Thanks for the history lesson, Ryan, but now is really not the fucking time, but you're not just a pretty face. I'll give you that." He grins, and all I see is the whites of his eyes and his sparkling white teeth as we continue our way up into the dark attic. I remove my knife from my rucksack as well as Sniper's favourite treats; the bag makes a rustling sound in my hand. We walk through the attic door shining our torches all around the room. I flick it backward when I spot some movement in the far corner and hear the sound of deep heavy breathing, spying a furry ass; Sniper's ass. He's fucking shagging something, someone. I get in closer, shaking the bag of dog treats and whistling. As I get to the corner of the room, I see the dirty bastard has a bloke pinned to the floor. His big, sharp white teeth are wrapped around his throat, and he's humping his fucking leg. "Sniper!" I shout, over-fucking-joyed he's OK. I burst into fits of laughter at what he's been up to.

Marcus actually fecking laughs. "Jesus, get his furry ass over here, will you?"

Once I get myself together again, I drag Sniper off the guy. I pound my fist into his face. "Next time, don't fucking bother trying to fuck with my boy, or I'll let him ass fuck you." His eyes grow wide as I lift my fist and punch him, knocking him clean out. "Hey, boy," I coo, giving Sniper's head a pat and feed him his treats.

"I can see why my son keeps you around." Marcus grins at me, his huge arms like his sons crossed over his broad chest.

"He's my brother," I say.

After I drop Marcus off at his house, I take Sniper home. Just as I get him in the door, my phone starts ringing. "Yeah?" I shout because the line is shite.

"There's no need to fucking yell, Ryan. It's Richie." His gruff voice comes down the line.

"Any news, mate?" I ask.

"We have a few leads; the plates are registered to a cottage out by Denholm, but we don't know for sure if Lee's in there."

"I'm on it." Killing the call, I put Sniper's food and water down then get back in my car. It's gonna be a long day.

THIRTY-THREE

Lee

It was pitch black when I woke up, and it stunk to high heaven of petrol. Even the light from under the door was out; it's been on the whole time I've been stuck in here. There mustn't be anyone else around. I feel for the rope tying my wrists together with my fingers. My wrists are sore from trying to untie them and from the rope being so fucking tight. Earlier I had had no choice but to stop, but now I'm fucking determined.

They will not keep me locked up in here while my girl's out there vulnerable. My fingers play around with the tight knot, and I manage to pull it looser. Breathing hard, I get up onto my feet. How do I get in these situations? I am trapped. I need to get the hell out. Just like fucking Houdini himself, I pull the knot free and get out of my restraints smiling like a Cheshire cat as I do. I charge the door to my now cell, my shoulder slamming into the hard, thick, wooden door. It doesn't budge an inch. Wrapping my hands around the door handle, I push and pull at it, but it still doesn't move. I step away from the door and charge at it again, hitting it full force with my right shoulder, my arm joints creaking with the huge pressure I put on the door. I roar out a final yell, and it shakes this time. I move my body further back to the wall at the back of the room and barge the door over and over, and suddenly it opens.

I'm met with a dimly-lit hallway, the lights from outside shining through the window. I click my shoulder back into place where the door had dislocated it. It hurts like a bitch, but the adrenaline coursing through me makes it bearable. I have no idea where I am as I move through the hallway. My blood boils underneath my flesh, fiery, my breathing becomes ragged as I start to move farther down the hall hoping with all that is in me the door I come to stand in front of isn't locked. I reach out my hand, wrapping it around the handle and turning it. I let out the breath I had been holding as I sigh in relief. The sound of the hallway door slamming echoes off the walls. My skin itches with the need to break free of this place. To get my revenge. And to get to Rose before they do.

My chest pumps with adrenaline. I roll up my sleeves and grit my teeth. The only thoughts occupying my mind as I navigated my way through the dark space are revenge. Someone is going to die painfully for this. I push my way through heading outside, my lungs burning with the fresh air I inhale deep into my lungs. I am finally free. I look behind me as the dark fog surrounds the building I had been locked up in, but I am close enough to make out an old farm house in the distance. Still, I have no idea where the fuck I am. I hear the sound of traffic, so I follow the noise in the distance, my feet hitting the ground hard as I sprint.

I move to the side and duck down in the field of long grass. Footsteps. I hear muffled footsteps, and they are heading toward me. Heavy boots hit the ground coupled with the sound of their deep breaths in and out as they run. I keep my head down, crouching on one knee, peering through the long blades of grass, scanning around me before I see them coming right toward me. Fuck! I throw my body forward using all the strength I have and tackle the man to the ground, pounding my fist into his balaclava-covered face. As we roll around on the ground, I don't stop until he pulls the cloth from his face. *Ryan.*

"Fuck, well that's nice, mate! Come to fucking break you out and you beat my ass to the fucking ground," he says, *grinning. Fucking grinning, the crazy bastard*. I could have killed him.

"Jesus, Ry, what the fuck are you doing? I've got this," I say, exasperated.
"Yeah, you keep saying that, and then you go and get yourself kidnapped." He pushes me back on my ass and grins like a loon. "I'm a fucking superhero. I came, and I rescued you. I'm the Irish

version of Superman except I'm better looking." He puts one arm up in the air like he is going to take off any second and runs forward, making whooshing sounds. Complete and utter loon.
"Whatever, mate, thanks for the semi-rescue, but can we get the fuck out of here?" I say.
He looks disappointed like I just told him to put his toys away. He punches me in the arm, and the pain shoots through me—he has a hard right hook. He doesn't know his own strength, and it doesn't help I'm already battered.
"Let's move," I say.
"Has anyone ever told you you need anger fucking management, Lee?" We start to run the way he came through the field.
"I've heard that once or twice, mate." I laugh, thinking of the last person who had told me exactly that.

Ryan lifts up his torch from the ground. He points it through the long grass then turns it off, sending us into blackness. "This way," he whisper-yells. Together we run, my ribs aching from the blows I took from those assholes as I suck in the cool night air, the sound of rushing blood swishing through my ears. I pant hard, my eyes staring forward into the dark field, my blurred eyes blinking hard as I fight to see. My stomach clenches thinking back on the last few hours. I hated being locked away, and now here I am sprinting to my freedom. Albeit beaten but not broken, my blood rages with revenge.

"You doing OK there, Lee? Nearly there, mate, I left the car hidden just under those trees." Ryan's head turns toward me as he speaks. We get to the edge of the trees on top of the hill and come to a stop. Ryan reaches out his arm, his hand coming around my shoulder.

"I'm good, Ry. You won't get rid of me that easily." I grin toward my friend who's giving me a man hug, patting me hard on my back. At this point in time, I'll take it; it's very much appreciated.

"Fucking good. You are my brother. I'll kill those fuckers for pulling this shit." He releases his hold on me, and we get into the car. Ryan reaches down, curling his tattooed hand around the lever and takes off the handbrake without starting the engine or putting on the lights. The car rolls down the hill, the only sound is both our panting breaths and the car wheels scraping against the gravel as it rolls slowly at first then speeds up when we reach the bottom. Only then does he start the engine. It roars to life. Hopefully there's no one around to alert. Keeping the lights off, we speed off into the dark winding roads. I realise we are out near Denholm Scottish borders to be exact.
"How the fuck did you manage to find me? We're out in the middle of fucking nowhere." I ask Ryan, looking out the car window.
"Tracked your phone," he says simply, turning a corner and out onto a busier road, switching on the headlights. Suddenly, a red Audi is closing in on the back of us, its engine roaring. It's them.
"Ry, they're behind us, put your foot down, mate." Ryan does but so do they, pushing right alongside us making Ryan swerve almost into the side the road.

"Fucking dicks!" he shouts. It doesn't stop there. One of them is hanging out of his window aiming his gun at us. Ryan puts his foot down harder moving the car away from their aim. The tires screech as Ryan swerves the car from side-to-side. And all I can do is sit here and watch. I look behind at the Audi, its lights glaring through the back window of Ry's car. Ryan's face mirrors my own; a look of pure anger and concentration. My eyes flicker back and forth to observe the car behind and to the wing mirrors. It weaves from side to side, and suddenly it pushes forward and crashes right into the back and pushes off to the side of the road. I automatically put my arms up in front of my head as the car rolls. It smashes into the barrier nearly cutting us in half. I think Ryan's knocked out, his seat belt holding him in place as we hang there upside down in our seats. The middle of the car behind our head is bent in half.

"Ryan, mate." I reach out to my closest friend seeing his head covered in blood. I don't know if he's still alive, but I have to get us the fuck out. I slip my hand into my jeans pocket frantically pulling at my phone. When I get it free I scroll numbers; Logan is the first number I see as he's the last person I had called.
"Come and get us, me and Ry have just been ran off the road," I whisper into the phone, my voice straining as the pain in my head starts to pound. I manage to give him a vague description of our whereabouts before succumbing to the blackness.

THIRTY-FOUR

Rose

I haven't seen Ryan yet; I've been so afraid of his reaction about my ex and his cronies attacking us, his good friend and himself. I've seen Lee nearly every day since he returned from being captured, and to say he's growing increasingly impatient with me is an understatement. It's like he can't bear to let me out of his sight. My excuses not to be with him are wearing thin. I see his frustrations every day. I cringe at my own shadow, and dark corners of my mind forever torment me. Never escaping my own demons. They beseech me with every turn. It has my heart in a vice squeezing the last dregs of a love I never thought I could have again. A love so deep for Lee, but how can I ever be free? Not just from Mike, but from my tormented mind. Will I ever find the happiness I crave? Will he ever leave me alone to let me raise our daughter? I want nothing more than to be by Lee's side, but I'm so afraid of what is to come.

I finish getting ready to drive over to Lee's. I need to talk to him. I need to tell him my fears and ask him what future he sees us having with everything hanging over our heads. The guilt I feel at the moment is unyielding, I cannot shake it off. A shiver tears up my spine. All of my instincts are on hyper-alert. Goosebumps prickle across my skin and my mind whispers incessantly that Mike is watching me. I shake myself. I am paranoid because I am nervous, but how do I tell the man that I'm in love with that it's over when he can see right through me? He sees deeper into my soul than anyone ever has. Being apart is the only way to keep us all safe.

On the drive over, I focus on the road, and I go over what I want to say to Lee in my head a thousand times. I abandon my car in front of the house and make my way inside the front door, my eyes squeezing shut as I rub the palms of my hands against my jeans. I'm so nervous they are turning sweaty. I don't want to do this, but I have to do this, I scream inside my mind. I stop in the middle of the hallway when the fear grips me. Should I turn back? I shouldn't have come here. I'm about to head back the way I came when I hear voices coming from the living room. I follow the sound and enter the room with the huge white sofa and the biggest windows I've ever seen. I love this room, sleek and light, a gangster's paradise, like the rest of the house. Not what you'd expect from a hardened criminal. Only those that are close enough to him know there's this whole other side, the side that's gentle, warm, protective and kind, the side I fell in love with. Much later, I fell in love with all of him.

"Hey, there you are." He's heading toward me, taking my hand. I give him a small smile as he leads me deeper into the room. He doesn't waste a second turning me in his arms and kissing me. I relax into the kiss and wrap my arms around his neck, all thoughts of everything I had planned to say gone in a second. And when he stops I grin, flushed red cheeks when the realisation there are others in the room hits me.

"Hey," I say shyly. Lee's sister Waff, Melissa, Logan, Dana and Ryan are here, and they're all smiling. How embarrassing, I think to myself. I walk toward the massive window; I still have that feeling and thoughts start racing through my mind that something bad is going to happen today. I can feel it in my bones. My heart picks up speed, and I rub at both of my arms with each hand. Everything inside me crumbling to ash, my heart is in disarray, I want to make my ex evaporate, I want the pain to end.
"Hey, put this on. Are you cold, baby? You're shivering." Lee's husky voice whispers in my ear from behind me slipping his hoodie around my shoulders and turning me to him. He sees everything.

"I'll be back soon, OK." I turn and watch him leave the room with Logan and Ryan.
"Come and sit down over here, chick." Dana pulls me toward the huge sofa, and I sit down beside her. Melissa and Waff join us, Sniper jumping up and planting himself in my lap, wagging his tail and licking my face.

"Good boy," I coo while stroking his soft, black and white head. It's as though he senses my anxiety—he's been through his own hell too. Just then, a bright, blinding light beams through the huge window. I stand and walk toward it, Sniper following me. His tail standing tall and pointed, his hackles up on end, staring out into the open space outside. Waiting and watching. The guys must be playing around with the security; I know we are pretty safe in here if the secure fences surrounding Lee's mansion are anything to go by.

"I need a drink. Anybody else want one? All this waiting around is making me thirsty." Waff said.

"Yeah, I could do with one thanks," I reply. Sniper looks at me then back to the window. He sits

down on his bum, his nose twitching trying to catch a scent of something, his eyes looking disappointed as he stares out into the lit-up grounds. "Hey, boy, it's all good. There are no bad people out there, I promise." I pat him on his soft, furry head and walk back over to where Dana is still sitting, and I take my place beside her again. "Where is Waff with those drinks? I hope Lee has something alcoholic, I could do with something pretty strong right now," I say, my nerves still sitting on edge.

"Me too, it's been a hell of a few months. The guys are on it. It will be sorted out soon, so don't worry." Dana clasps her fingers together in her lap as she speaks. Looking at her closer, I can see the tension written all over her too.

"I promise you this, all this pain, all this worry, our lives being turned upside down? The deep fear that eats at both you and me day in day out? It will disappear." I lean into her, wrapping my arms tightly around her for a hug.

"Oh well, isn't that sweet?" Melissa is standing directly in front of us, a weird grin on her face. She keeps talking. "You're such close friends, and it's quite cute." She pauses, looking from me to Dana then back again. "But, Rose, you know you aren't good enough for Lee, right?" She mocks, crossing her arms over her chest one hip to the side.

"What?" Dana glares at her. I stare in disbelief at her words, self-doubt creeping right into my already messed up mind. I can't believe my ears. How dare she?

"And what's that supposed to mean?" I question just as Waff comes back into the room with a bottle of tequila and four shot glasses.

"Melissa, don't be such a bitch. Just ignore her; she's been in love with my brother since forever. Nobody is good enough for Lee in her eyes. It's nothing against you personally." She pours out four shots of tequila. I throw mine back letting the warm liquid slide down my throat, the warmth spreading through my body calming down my frantic nerves.

"Hey, I'm not a bitch!" She glares at me. "But nobody is good enough for my boy Lee, isn't that right, Katerina?" Melissa spits.

"I'm warning you now, Melissa, don't start your shit with me. Friend or not I'll put you on your ass," Waff shouts. Melissa sighs and slumps down in an empty chair, swiping tequila as she does.

We have a few more shots and chat about day-to-day things. The more I drink, the better I relax and forget about the uneasy feeling coiling in my gut. And then I hear his voice, all the blood draining from my face and that ever-present panic resurfacing. Oh, shit.

"Now, now, bitches. Calm the fuck down." Standing in the doorway, his voice cuts through me like ice as he throws me the most contemptuous look I've ever seen. "Rose, what have I told you

about drinking alcohol? You know I don't like it. Yet here you are, the whore that you are drinking with your little whore friends."

"I'm so sorry, Mike, I never thought…" I mumble, looking around at my friends. The sight of him standing in Lee's living room absolutely terrifies me.

"You're sorry?" he shouts. "What? You never thought I'd find out? What are you thinking of, Rose? I am your husband, and you have betrayed me in the worst possible way. Trust me, you'll be punished accordingly."

I fall toward the sofa behind me unable to stand any longer as his twisted evil face glares at me. I shake with fear gripping my heart like a vice. The room falls deathly silent for several long minutes when Waff moves toward Mike, and she asks, "How did I do? Have I done well?"

I turn toward Dana, and her facial features mirror my own—utter shock and devastation. Lee's own sister has betrayed us all. I can't believe my ears or eyes.

"Yes, darling, very well indeed." He curls his huge arm around the front of her throat and pulls her forward, kissing her roughly on the lips. All the time, his eyes stay on me. Melissa moves to their side, smiling at Dana and me. The bitch was in on it too.

Mike walks over to the door, and he locks it. "He has a key?" I whisper out loud to Dana.

"So cocky and confident, aren't we, ladies? You're not so cocky now, are you?" Melissa laughs and points at us like a stupid crazed lunatic, her eyes wide, a smug look covering her face making her seem ugly. I pull Dana to her feet and move us back away from them to the window. "You're nothing to him, Rose, do you hear me? Do you understand? He's just using you. He can smell the whore in you." Her cackle grates on my ears, loud and shrill and definitely crazy.

"I love him." My confession to my ex-husband sparks his anger tenfold. He takes a step toward me, making me take a step back which just riles him further.

"So, you think that man loves you back?" He laughs a deep rumbling laugh. "Yes, he does, I know he does," I say, sure in my conviction.

"No, my dear wife, he does not fucking love you!" He shouts in my face, spittle hitting my cheeks as he rants. "Are you that blind you can't see he's just using you for a fuck whenever he feels like it? Why would another man want a worthless whore like you?" Tears sting my eyes. I try hard not to let his words cut me in two, but I can't, and I can't hold back the river of tears starting to fall.

"Stop it, you piece of shit! Don't talk to her like that. She's not a whore, and she's a far better person than you will ever be," Dana says, holding my hand so tightly in hers as she speaks, her voice bold and brave.

"You—" he points at Dana "—are just as bad if not worse than my wife!" Mike spits.

Thirty-Five

Dana

No fucking way, this is not happening. It just can't be. I'm dreaming, no wait—I'm drunk. That explains the hallucinations I'm having right at this very moment. It's the bloody shots. I cannot get over that bitch—two bitches. My hands are scrunched up so tight my nails are scratching the skin on my palms. How could they do this? Why are they doing this to us? They know what we had been through with these type of animals, they know how dangerous these men are. We have opened up so many times and explained the torment. I opened up to Melissa. I had cried. Actually broke down in front of her. I gave her a job for fuck's sake.

I turn my head to look at Rose seeing the fear clear in her eyes—her face has turned as white as snow. It's petrifying to look at her. She has come so far since we came to the Scottish Borders even though it had taken a while for her and Annie to settle down and to feel safe again, rebuild their lives. And although it took even longer for her and Lee to get together, she had finally managed to let go of some of the demons that haunt her mind daily. I stare at her. I just hope that the guys get here soon. Where are they?

I move my hand and run it down Rose's arm until I reach her hand. I squeeze it, whispering into her ear, "Everything will be OK." Her eyes fill with terror and disbelief as she looks into mine. Without speaking, she nods her head a few times, but I know that she doubts my words. I feel it when her body starts to shake next to me. Her ex-husband stands before us with evil seeping from every part of him. Without being able to stop myself, I launch my body forward jumping onto Melissa's back, wrapping my arms as tightly as I can around her scrawny little neck.

"Get off me, you stupid bitch, what do you think you're doing?" she screams, but I don't let go of her. I can't. I am like an angry hissing cat, my sharp claws scratching at the sick little mouse beneath me, my nails swiping across the skin on her face. I hold on tighter, my thighs wrapping around her body to keep a strong hold, my hands ripping out her hair.

"You! Why did you do this to her? She's my friend, she's your friend. How could you do this? We gave you everything, we let you in, I let you in. You know what we have been through, you twisted evil bitch." My rage explodes further, my fist pounding into the side of her head anywhere I can strike out and hurt her like she hurt my friend.

"Get off me!" she shouts as I continue to punch her in the head.

"Stop this now!" a voice booms in my ears as I am pulled from Melissa's back by Mike, but the voice isn't his.

Thirty-Six

Rose

From the corner, in the dark shadows of the room, Dana's ex-husband Ian steps out. Evil coats his tongue as he speaks. "And there she is. Who are you? Not the woman I married, but you still belong to me, and I'm taking you home." He grins at Dana who visibly shakes at my side. We are trapped like wild rabbits cornered by vicious dogs. I can't help but wonder where the fuck our guys are.

"Over my dead body you are!" I tell him.

"That can be arranged," Melissa says, moving to Ian's side. She leans in and kisses him on the cheek. Dana and I both suck in air, unable to breathe, unable to believe what is happening here. In Lee's house, no less. I start to scream, but like lightning, Mike has me by the throat, his other hand covering my mouth as he begins sniffing my hair. Ian has Dana pinned to the floor with her hands held behind her back. He ties her wrists together and gags her so she can't scream for help. Mike removes his tight grip from around my mouth.

I plead with him, "Please let us go." The tears are falling down my cheeks, my words now cries

—begging cries. I beg so hard, but to no avail. Mike runs his hand down the front of my throat. It travels its way down to the neckline of my tee which he tears away from my body. He continues to run his hand over me, along the side of my breast. Then he tears away my bra and starts to knead at my breasts with both hands, his length digging into my back as it grows with his need. I feel disgusted as I am suddenly pushed up against Mellissa. She pulls off my jeans and throws them aside. I am bared to all standing in just my knickers. I glare long and hard at Melissa as she smirks at me, eyeing me up and down. My skin crawls, but I promise myself that I won't crumble. That someone will come, and this will all be over soon.

Mike's hands grope at my breasts rough and hard, his fingers pinching at my nipples making them go hard much to my disgust. I feel sick at his touch yet I can't move, I can't scream, I can't do anything but stand rooted to the spot and let him torture me. He twists me around to face him, his eyes roaming all over my body, his left hand gripping the back of my hair tightly pulling back my head. Yanking me forward, he slips his right hand into my knickers and slides a finger deep inside me. "You and this pussy are mine. They belong to me. You hear me, bitch?" He thrusts his finger in and out roughly making my body shake, the pain he is causing makes vomit crawl up my throat, a whimper slipping from my lips. He mistakes it as a sign I am enjoying it and leers down at me.

"Enough of this, this is not the plan." Waff steps forward. Mike releases me and my hands instinctively cover up my exposed chest. I run over to the window putting distance between him and me.

"Plan?" He laughs. "The plan was what I say it was, bitch. You forget your place, little girl." Waffs body flies across the room, her back hitting the coffee table, the force of Mike's punch and hitting the table making her scream out in pain. "Pathetic little whore, trying to play with the big boys, huh?" he snarls at her.

Leaning over her, he takes her head in his hands, gives a sharp twist and snaps her neck, her lifeless body slipping back down onto the table. I gasp and start backing up toward the glass of the window watching Melissa coming toward me with a big sharp knife in her hands, the silver blade so shiny in the light it reflect into my eyes and blinding me for a couple of seconds. My back hits the cold window, and then I feel the blade slicing through my skin, a sharp pain shooting through my stomach three times. I look down at the blood pouring out of me. The blade is covered in blood.

I lift my head and look into Melissa's eyes. "What did you do?" I ask.

Shaking my head from side to side vigorously, I press blood-covered hands as hard as I possibly can into the wounds still pouring with blood. Slicing pain shoots through me so blinding that I can't tell where it starts and where it ends. I look up and search around the room for Lee, but my eyes land on Mike's wide green eyes. Shock covers his face when the horror of the vicious attack by Melissa's hands dawns on him.

"Lee." My voice is barely a whisper. All I can see is Lee's beautiful face, all I can hear is his husky voice as my eyes flutter to a close. "I love you."

EPILOGUE

"Security breach, Lee, on the west side. Camera five. Brave motherfuckers." Ryan turns in his seat, his eyes wide and darkening with anger.

"Ry, what the fuck, who?" I ask, looking at the screen.

"I can't make out who it is. Their faces are covered in masks. Looks like they're carrying, mate," he tells me, standing and slipping on his bulletproof vest, a pile of them sitting at his feet underneath the desk.

"They can't crack their way in here, we're pretty safe, Ry," I say.

Ryan picks up another vest from under the desk and throws it at me. "Better being safe than having a sorry holey ass. Even Irish superheroes don't need bullets in their butt," he says. I grin.

"I'm sure you would find a way to enjoy that shit, Ry." I slip on my vest, loving that my friend and brother never fails to lighten the mood in a fucked up situation.

"I've called Declan; he's two hours away, but he will be here as soon as he can," Logan says, fastening up his vest. "We better get moving before those fuckers try to come through those doors." Whoever they are better not set foot near my woman. Jesus', the fucking brass balls of them!"

We pick up pace and dart through the house, the long hallway that runs the length of downstairs is eerily quiet as we approach the closed doors of the living room. I give Ryan a worried look and then ram my foot into the door, underneath the handle to dislodge the lock. It budges a fraction the first time, so I kick harder the second, the door swinging inward and banging on the wall behind.

I have to break down my own living room door. Pointing my gun inside the deathly silent room as I slowly walk forward, Ryan and Logan at my back, the sight that greets us boils the blood in my veins. I struggle to comprehend what I'm looking at, my heart beating violently in my chest. My sister is lying there dead on the coffee table. I can tell she's already gone by the milky hue of her eyes as she stares right through me, void of all breath. My legs shiver; I am unable to stand any longer. I lean against the wall as the vomit crawls up my throat and empties onto the floor.

It takes me a long moment to compose myself, but when I do I look around the room, I catch sight of Mellissa standing, staring toward the wall, her face and hair bloodied. I can't see what she's looking at for now. I move farther into the room and spot Dana lying on the floor behind the sofa, rubbing at her wrists, rope still attached where she had obviously been tied up. I lean down toward her, still aiming my gun at the centre of the room until I see Logan sprinting through the now broken window, the glass shattered, a huge hole like the one I can feel in my heart. Ryan makes his way around the room scanning every corner. I untie the rest of the rope from around Dana's wrist. Her restraints haven't kept her down for long. She reaches out her arms and grips herself onto my side shaking and sobbing.

She looks directly into my eyes. "They were all in on it together, Lee. Mellissa, your sister—they were going to try and take us away," she whimpers. I could only stare at her trying to get my head around her words.

Rubbing my hand down her hair, I tell her it's OK. "Shhh, it's OK. You're OK, Dana." I pull her tighter into my side.

"Melissa killed Rose." A harsh sob escapes her mouth, and I gasp. "She's dead, Lee. She's dead." Dana points to the end of the sofa, her hand shaking as she continues to cry.

I stand, and what I see rips out my soul completely. Ryan has his fingers on Rose's neck yet he's looking at me in an odd way, a way that silently tells me that she has gone. The room suddenly starts to blur. I take a sharp gulp of breath, shaking uncontrollably as I try to suck the air into my lungs. I'm frozen in place. My brain is spinning inside my head. I can't stop shaking. I can't make sense of anything at all. I'm in a black hole trying to claw my way back out.

"Rose," I call. I start to chant her name, but she can't hear me. *"Rose."* I crumble to the floor onto my knees. *"Rose,"* I cry again, my heart disintegrating, a million tiny pieces shattering in the air around me.
I can't breathe. *"Rose."*
It's agony, sheer agony that slices the very core of me. Seeing her lifeless, bloodied body lying on the floor bared to the world. I feel so helpless. I feel so weak. The overpowering emotion making me remember that I had let myself be human again. But I am not weak even with the tears starting to flood down my face, and as if my mind goes completely numb, all I see is red. I lift my gun and without a second thought put a bullet into Mellissa. Her head flies back, her body slumping where she stood, before the vomit spills from my mouth onto the floor.

Surviving You

Katerina's funeral was held in a small funeral home, but it was filled with family members. Family members who had no idea what my sister had gotten herself into. I resented all of those people grieving for her; if only they knew the ugly truth of who she really was. I resented that I had to stand strong. When my heart was crushed, the darkness had clouded over in my mind; any light that remained was now extinct. My dad didn't want them all to know she had turned traitor, turned on her own flesh and blood. My dad tried hard to hold it together yet he fell apart within minutes of the service starting. I held onto him. I supported him as best as I could even though I couldn't cry for my baby sister. I was still so angry. Her betrayal helped me losing the only light I had ever had in my life. No, I couldn't grieve for my sister. I could only grieve for Rose. A woman I'll never stop loving until the day that I die. A woman whose life I will avenge when that time comes, I will not take my last breath until justice is served and all those responsible are in the ground. It still sets me off thinking that the fuckers managed to cause so much mayhem in such a short space of time and then disappear out of a fucking window like a puff of goddamned smoke. Yet I hold onto the knowledge that their day will come, and it will be at my hand.

The morning of Rose's funeral comes, and God has opened up the heavens. It's pouring down with rain, and it feels like I'm being pissed on some more. The rain falls, hiding my tears that continue to stream down my face. The dark clouds cover the sky; the thunder rolls like the devil himself will be here any second. And I will gladly go with him straight to the dark depths of hell where I belong. The wind whips against my face bringing with it the sting of a loss that I will never come back from.

Dana and Logan are quiet; they have been taking care of little Annie. Dembie and Mandy haven't said much at all and Ryan is handling things better than anyone else, keeping it together and taking control. He's even managed to track down the rest of Rose's family, but they had refused to make the journey, refused a place for Annie to go to, their own flesh and blood. But that's their loss—little Annie is better off staying here surrounded by the people she loves and love her.

As we stand outside the old church, the mood is somber. There's nothing but sadness in the air. Annie hasn't spoken a single word since she heard the news that her mum had died. I take her small hand in mine, and she looks up at me, her big brown eyes just like her mum's are tired looking, red and blotchy, filled with fresh tears, the pain clear on her face.

"Annie, little Annie." I almost choke on the lump in my throat. It makes my voice break.

"Is Mummy sad now in heaven? Like when my dad used to always make her sad?" she asks, her innocence not lost on me. "I drew her this picture so that she will never forget me. Do you think she will like it?" Sweet, heartbroken Annie hands me a folded up piece of paper she removed from a pink envelope. "This is me, Mummy, and you holding hands in the park and those are daffodils—her favourite flowers."
I look down at Annie's picture, and I read her small handwriting, my heart aches all over again.

To my mummy, I hope that this will make you very happy. Please don't forget me, and please don't ever be sad. I love you forever. Love, Annie x

The End
Look out for more from Lee and Ryan's story in 2016.

A note to the reader

Dear reader,
I am a domestic abuse survivor.
I used to think myself worthless to be treated so badly by my ex-partner. I used to believe that the beatings I received and that the mental torture I endured, I deserved. I believed it was my own fault that he treated me this way. I shouldn't have made him angry; I shouldn't have opened my mouth to speak because every time I did it was the wrong thing to say. I shouldn't wind him up. I should do as I'm told. I should obey his every command. But even doing this it was always the wrong thing. Always wrong. Nothing that I could say or do was ever the right thing in his eyes. It gets you to a point where you feel you can't fall any lower, that you may as well be dead.

What would it matter if he did kill me? In my head it would have been better than living with the constant fear inside my heart it tore me up. You get used to the beatings, but the mental torture is what scars you the most; believing that you are worth nothing, believing that nobody else will love you or ever could.

But now I know that I am not worthless. I didn't deserve to be beaten; I didn't deserve to be made to feel like I wanted to die, to end the pain. Now though I believe that you can do anything when you put your mind to it, and you should never be scared of any other human being no matter how much they try to put the fear god into you. You are worth so much more and anything is possible. I still have days where I struggle; but I found myself again, and I finally believe in me.

If you, or if you know of anyone that is going through some kind of domestic abuse be it mental physical or both then please don't let that person push you away. Or you yourself are going through it then please contact someone talk to someone if you feel you can't talk to anyone you know or feel ashamed then please don't be you're not alone. There's helplines you can contact there is an army of people out there waiting to help even if you just want to talk you don't even have to give your name if you don't feel comfortable but please don't live in silence.

Free phone line 0808 2000 247 UK
https://www.victimsupport.org.uk/?
1-800-799-7233 | 1-800-787-3224 (TTY) USA
http://www.thehotline.org/ Australia (03) 9486 9866
Or google Domestic abuse helpline.

ACKNOWLEDGEMENTS

Thank you to my family and friends who sacrifice their time so I can write and bring these stories to life. I love you with all of my heart. Thank you to everyone who buys, reads, promotes, stalks and helps me get my stories out there I cannot thank you all enough. To my street team and to the blogs - thank you for everything you do, you're all awesome, hardworking and an amazing support. You are the people who keep me writing so thank you from the bottom of my heart.
Street Team/Beta readers.

Klaire Sutherland, Clare Roden, Ashley Gibbons, Jane Deeney, Sarah Payne, Lisa Cullinan, Michelle Booklover Simm, Lj Knox, Debbie Talbot, Kim Tatum, Virginia Tesi Carey, Hilary Suppes, Debbie Boffey, Shona Reid, Amber Starr, Paige Rymer, Louise Mckie, Summer Clarke. I love you all to the moon and back. You're all amazing friends, I'm so glad you came into my life. I don't know how you put up with me. Dmb drawings thank you for the amazing drawing for the cover you know how much I love it and you. Cover designer is the amazing Melissa at MGBookcovers. Formatting Wendi Lynne.

Klaire how can I put into words and say thank you. The hours you have spent with me on this. You are priceless to me. I know that I have probably given you a headache and I've given you a few moments where you probably thought I was crazy. You're a great friend an angel and an ever constant support, and I love you.

Wendi Lynn Thank you so much for the tough love that you have shown me that I need. I hope to work with you on other projects in the near future. And thank you for putting up with me.

Jodi Marie Maliszewski - Thank you for being you; you put a smile on my face every single day without even knowing you're doing it.

ww.facebook.com/groups/SurvivingYou/
www.facebook.com/groups/DawnsDiamondDollsOfficialStreetTeam/

Surviving You

PLAYLIST

Tupac Dear Mamma Pharrell Williams Happy
Bump & Grind Waze and Odyssey & R, Kelly
Bob Marley Don't worry about a thing
P, Diddy Missing You Luniz I got 5 on it Tupac Changes
Wiz-Khalifa See You Again ft. Charlie Puth
Calvin Harris & Disciples-How deep is your Lost Frequencies Are You With Me
Ice cube You Can Do It U2 Every Breaking Wave
I will Never Let You Down Rita Ora Loyal Chris Brown
Pills N Potions Nicki Minaj Stay With Me Sam Smith All Of Me John Legend Waves Mr. Probz Na Na Trey Songz
She came to give it to you Usher Are You With Me Lost Frequencies Run Away (U & I) Galantis Rihanna - Hate That I Love You ft. Ne-Yo
Justin Timberlake - What Goes Around...Comes Around Light Em' Up Centuries - Fall Out Boy
Taylor Swift – Style Three Days Grace – Pain Maroon 5 - One More Night
Jason Derulo - "Want To Want Me" Maroon 5 – Maps
BOB MARLEY FEAT LAURYN HILL "Turn your lights down low" Nickelback - Savin Me

Justin Timberlake – SexyBack Someone Like You - Van Morrison Breaking Benjamin - I Will Not Bow Luke Bryan - Play It Again
Beast of burden by the rolling Stones
Jessie J, Ariana Grande, Nicki Minaj - Bang Bang ft. Ariana… Sam Smith - Lay Me Down
Rihanna - Hate That I Love You ft. Ne-Yo Hello Adele
Pia Mia - Do It Again ft. Chris Brown, Tyga Simply Red - Holding Back The Years Brandy – Baby
TLC – Creep

TLC – Waterfalls
Brandy & Monica - The Boy Is Mine Lauryn Hill - Doo-Wop
Mary J. Blige - Be Without You Mary J. Blige - No More Drama Mary J. Blige - Take Me As I Am Mary J. Blige - Share My World
2Pac - Wonda Why They Call U Bitch Feat. Faith Evans 2Pac - Everyday Struggle (Hold On Be Strong)
2Pac - Till We Meet Again
2Pac feat. Faith Evans - I'll Be Missing You Eminem - Not Afraid
K Klass - Rhythm Is A Mystery Eminem - When I'm Gone Eminem - Like Toy Soldiers Eminem – Beautiful
Eminem – Mockingbird Eminem - Without Me
Snoop Dogg - Gangstas Don't Live That Long Dr. Dre, Snoop Dogg - Nuthin' But A G Thang 2Pac - Holler If Ya Hear Me
2pac - I Ain't Mad At Cha Liquid - Sweet Harmony Ultracynic - Nothing Is Forever

About the author

I was brought up in Manchester and I am now living in the beautiful Scottish borders with my three children.

I have enjoyed writing my story as I had a pretty hard upbringing and have suffered like everyone does over the years in different situations, but everyone has a story to tell.

I just hope my story can help someone out there who is, or has been through the same sorts of situations as myself.

Follow me:
Facebook Tsu Twitter

Other books by Dawn A Keane
Surviving Him

Dawn A Keane

SURVIVING HIM

Copyright © 2015 Dawn Keane
All rights reserved.

No part of this book may be reproduced or transmitted in any form or by any means, electronic or mechanical, including photocopying, recording, or by any other information storage and retrieval system without the written permission of the author, except in the case of brief quotations embodied in critical articles and reviews.
This book is a work of fiction, all names, characters, places, and events are the products of the author's imagination, or are used fictitiously. Any resemblance to actual persons, living or dead, events, or locations is entirely coincidental.
All rights reserved. Except as permitted under the UK Copyright, Designs and Patents Act 1988.

Surviving You

Prologue

The Women's Aid worker, Pam, seems like a kind lady with short, blonde hair, and concerned grey eyes as she sits opposite me behind her desk with a sympathetic look on her face. A pen and a notebook are situated in front of her and she is listening to my every word, while I tell her of the abuse I suffered at the hands of my ex-husband. All because of a bloody tap.

I turned the tap on as slowly as I could to fill up the kettle, and the water pipe made a loud screeching sound, a rumbling that shook through the whole house. It did that every time the tap was turned on. Ian was in bed and it woke him up. He was so angry with me, he jumped out of the bed, ran down the stairs towards me and started having a complete meltdown, going completely ballistic at me for waking him up. I shook with fear his as his eyes blazed with anger; a murderous violence poured from him as he glared down at me. He started shouting at me for turning the tap on the wrong way. He said that I was a stupid fool for not knowing how do it properly. I didn't realize there was a right way to do it. I was so frightened because I knew what was coming next.

Ian lost it completely and flew at me so fast my head spun. He was shouting and swearing; he was beyond being in control of his temper. I was scared out of my mind. I trembled as my throat closed. I proceeded to beg him not to hurt me. I pleaded with him, but it didn't do any good. He flew at me again and punched me so hard in the face that I fell on my knees on the floor. Ian didn't want to hear anything I had to say. He got right in my face with his forehead firmly pressed up against mine, pushing me down and shaking me with the force. "You're pathetic. You don't even know how to do a simple thing. Not knowing how to turn on a tap quietly, you stupid bitch." He punched me again and again. "Next time, yeah," he shouted, "Do it fucking right." He punched me on the right side of my jaw. I could no longer hold myself up.

I slowly agreed that I was pathetic for not knowing how to turn the damn tap on correctly, then my head smashed on the floor full force.

I could feel the blow to my eyes as he repeatedly hit me over and over and again. Black spots filled my vision then everything turned black. When I came to, I couldn't believe what was happening to me, and Kayleigh. Was she ever going to be safe? What sort of mum am I to let this happen? How can I stop it? I believed that I must have deserved everything I went through. I must have one of those faces men want to injure. Ian left me alone and went to his sister's house to calm down. I went to the bathroom and splashed my face with cold water, and it hurt so much I winced; the pain was excruciating. The water slowly soothed my face, stinging slightly with each splash. I couldn't see very well as my eyelids had swelled and were changing colour, my tears stinging the open wounds. My head was in so much pain, I put my face back into the water in the sink to soothe it.

I looked up into the mirror; I was a complete mess. No amount of make-up was going to cover it up; it felt like my heart would pop through my chest, it was racing so hard.

All I wanted to do was go and see my mum and tell her what happened, ask her for help. But I knew she would be disappointed in me. I couldn't call her and tell her, she would think I'm such a failure. I stared at my broken reflection in the mirror trying to figure out what I had done to deserve this and I couldn't. I was so shocked, so scared out of my mind. Ian was back in no time at all with a box of chocolates, like that made it all ok again. He said he was a psychotic human being. He kept saying how sorry he was, so sorry for what he had done, so sorry for losing control and that he couldn't believe he had hurt his woman. He promised me it would never happen again, but the damage was already done.

Chapter One

I'm having one of those moments: the milk-in-the-cupboard, sugar-in-the-fridge moments. On any given day, I can catch my coat pocket, or whatever I'm wearing on a door handle, a cupboard, or anything really. If it has a handle or anything that sticks out, it is guaranteed to grab me and pull me straight off my feet and onto my clumsy ass. This might be my best inept performance yet.

"Damn, I'm clumsy as fuck!"

As of now, I have dropped the hair dryer onto my foot and I've recently fractured my big toe on a heavy wooden door, while chasing my friend's ten-year-old son in a tea towel fight. Hopefully, this puts me at my quota for unnecessary injuries for the week.

"Now are you sure you have got everything you need sweetie? Have you packed your phone charger? I need to be able to reach you. Your onesie; you need to take it. It's bloody freezing in Scotland and you'll need a warm coat."

Rose sits on the end of my bed looking at my suitcase stuffed full of things I don't even need. You would think I was about to move to the other side of the world the way she is eyeing me.

"I think so and it's not that cold in Scotland." I couldn't help the smile that was spreading across my face at her concern for me. It's July for God sake. "Hey, I'm only going to Edinburgh for a few days, it's not that far away, and I'll be back here before you know it."

I throw down my hair straighteners that I held onto in my other hand and sit down on the bed beside her. I take her hand in mine; she knows how worried I am about traveling alone with the girls.

"I know, but I'm really going to miss you guys, and it's Scotland you're going to. It feels like it's so far away to me and I will worry." She speaks in a soft tone, as she struggles to come to terms with me going away. We have become so close living here together; five women in one house, sharing a bond like no other. We share everything. I stand and zip up my case and throw myself into her arms for a hug. As tears slide down her cheeks, she turns toward the door. When she reaches it, she turns her head towards me and smiles.

"Don't do anything I wouldn't do."

I mirror her warm smile and state, "As if."

The door closes.

Hobbling around, I've managed to pack my case with all the essentials that us girls need for our trip. We will be leaving our hometown in Manchester and heading up to Edinburgh. My most critical accessories for this trip are definitely my wedges. If you ever have the misfortune of breaking your big toe, having several pairs of killer wedges in your wardrobe is a life-saving must-have.

We ride the metro train into Manchester. "You poor girls must be so embarrassed with me hobbling along beside you, I can't believe my luck," I say to the girls, in apology for my slowing our progress.

I'm so stupid. I amaze myself at how clumsy I can be. We make it onto the train okay; I watch, as people are busy, rushing around to get on or off the train. The noises around us makes me smile; loud voices echo around the platform, the sound of the trains chugging past, stopping to pick people up and take them to their destination. I bring my head back inside the train, and the door automatically closes.

"Mum, can we sit here, please?" Amy beams up at me from the seat she has found with a table in the middle.

"We have the best seats on the train, Amy," I tell her while Kayleigh and I take our seats next to her. We were really doing this; making memories, good ones, instead of remembering all the bad things, the nightmare that is our life living in fear and always on the run from my ex-husband. The man starts checking doors on the train further down the platform; we watch him through the window. A man's voice emanates through the speakers telling us to have a great journey and thanks us for traveling with Virgin trains.

Looking out of the train window as the buildings rush past my eyes, I have to look away before I go completely cross-eyed. My girls play super Mario on their Nintendo's until they eventually fall asleep. The chugging sound of the train is kind of relaxing, and I fall asleep too. I wake to the sight of beautiful green trees, and a green landscape that stretches out for miles. It is just sheer beauty in front of our eyes. I know we are in Scotland; those trees are like thousands of Christmas trees standing tall and proud. The air is cooler and fresher; even stuck inside the train I could feel it.

Both Kayleigh and Amy are so excited; it is going to be an amazing few days. Our journey is to celebrate Kayleigh's tenth birthday; I can't believe how fast she's growing up. She's so beautiful; big, dark blue eyes like mine, and long brown hair. It feels like yesterday that she was born, which also happened to be the first day of the opening of the Scottish Parliament. This year, she has been invited to join in at Holyrood for the Scottish Parliament's tenth anniversary celebrations, joining up with all the other kids that were born on that day in Scotland.

As part of the celebration, she will also get to meet the Queen of England. Perfectly awesome. I have their dresses all picked out, elegant matching little pale pink maxi ball gown-style. I adore these little dresses so much, if only they had them in my size.

"Damn, you two will look so sweet all dressed up. Unquestionably beautiful."

I got them both matching shoes and all the accessories a girl could ever need.

My dress is black and silver satin with small crystals along the neckline, cut over one shoulder and sits nicely above my knees. I have a black tiny clutch to match that just barely fits my phone, if I'm lucky. And because of my stellar walking skills, I get to finish off my outfit with my killer black life-saver wedges that I had to literally hop out and buy in a rush just before we went to the station this morning.

We arrive in Edinburgh safe and sound. There are so many things about the city of Edinburgh that I love: the old buildings and architecture, the history of the region, and the majestic Edinburgh Castle. It really is exquisite. The sounds of this city, always buzzing with life; it's magical.

Manchester and Edinburgh, even though they are only about a hundred and seventy miles apart, are two cities that have entirely different cultures; their histories inter-woven, but uniquely individual. I love the contrasts and being able to experience it all within just a few hours journey.

One of my favourite things about Scotland is the smell of the fresh ocean air coming off the North Sea. Scotland has the freshest tap water I've ever tasted. I don't know what it is, but I can only imagine that it must be because of the year-round rains that replenish the region's fresh surface water sources. Everyone raves about it; it's delicious, and you just can't beat it.

"I need to remember to bottle some of that and take it home with me."

"Seriously, Mum." Kayleigh gave me a huge smile. She thinks I'm mental, in a good kind of way.

"I love it. It's the freshest water there is anywhere, it's so good!"

"Mum, you're crazy you know that, right?" She gives me a stare like I'm losing my marbles. Apparently, she doesn't share my love of the crisp sweetness that is fresh Scottish tap water. "Mum, I don't think you're allowed to take Scottish water away from Scotland, it might be against the law." Amy gives me a look that shuts me up about my nonsensical thoughts on the water in Scotland.

I raise my palms up in the air. "Ok, no water in bottles."

A taxi is waiting for us as we exit the train station. Although they enjoyed the train ride, Kayleigh and Amy are starting to get tired and can't wait to get to the hotel and freshen up. I'll just say they are, well, a bit pissed off after a long day of traveling.

We check into the hotel, and we are shown to our lovely room. It's a nice size space with two massive beds that would easily fit a family of six. While the girls explore our suite and unpack their bags, my thoughts drift back home to Manchester.

Our life at home isn't as glamorous. Our daily lives are filled with fear for our safety, living in a women's refuge, a shelter for women who have suffered domestic abuse, still on the run, still hiding from the threat of mentalist ex-husbands; mine being, Ian. I share this rather matter-of-factly, but, to be honest, it's simply that we've lived this way for so long now, it's just become our reality; a life I never thought I would be living.

Life in the refuge can be amazingly hard on your soul at times; lacking a sense of direction, not knowing which way you're heading or which way to turn next, or who to turn to. I don't want to bother people with my troubles, so we've just got to stick it out. I try to be as strong as I can for my babies.

They are the most important precious things in the world to me. Nothing will come between us, and I will protect them with my life. I just wish that they had a proper family life, a home with none of this shit, this upheaval, not knowing whether we are coming or going. They surprise me though; no matter what is thrown at them, they take it and just get on with things. I'd hate to think what is going on in their heads, and how this situation will affect them later on in their lives when they start having their own relationships.

My darling Amy; she adores her dad and unfortunately for me things didn't work out with Amy's dad, Logan. Our relationship was ruined by the burden of my issues from my abusive marriage. I love Amy's father to pieces, my second husband-to-be in my dreams. I love him with every part of my soul and I always will. He's been so good to us all, even when he injured his leg and had to leave the armed forces; all he worried about was the girls and me. We lost our home; he eventually went to recover at his mum and dad's house after spending a long time in the hospital. It was torture not being able to see or speak to him. I thought I had lost him, but I ended up losing him in a different way anyway. It wasn't possible for us to live together in Scotland. My ex-husband made sure of that, and if I had tried to stay with Logan, Ian would have tracked us down. So I had no choice but to leave the man I wanted to spend the rest of my life with and everything that I knew where we were happy - home.

"Remind me to text your dad, Amy, so he knows we're safe."

"I will, Mum, and tell him I love him and miss him."

"Sure will, chick. He loves you, and Kayleigh, too, sweetheart," I remind her as I kiss her on the nose. I call and text him every day, but I haven't had a reply as of yet. I keep in touch with his parents when I can. Logan's on his road to recovery so that's more than I could ever wish for, he's alive. My sex life (when I had one) with Logan was insanely amazing. I had my first real orgasm, as in, eyes-rolling-in-the-back-of-my-head, toe-curling, most incredible orgasm EVER. Getting to know every inch of my body, his experienced hands found all my sensitive spots with confidence. He isn't shy in the slightest, and he made me feel things I hadn't felt; worshiping my body like he was touching my soul and wrapping it around his heart.

Chapter Two

I think back to my time with Logan. I met him properly in a local bar while I was living in a little town in Scotland. I had seen him around town; he was unbelievably sexy, and everyone seemed to take notice of him. So attractive you could see he worked out all the time. And when I looked into those eyes I wanted to wrap myself around him and live there. We crossed paths from time to time; at the market, or the pub, or at a party in the small town we lived in called Jedburgh in the Scottish borders. Until one day, while I was sitting in a pub with a few friends from work, Logan came up to me and asked me out on a date.

"Alright, Dana?"

I knock back the rest of my drink and sputtered out my response to him. "Hey, Logan. How are you doing?" I was afraid that I'd made a sloppy fool of myself, and tried to wipe away my drink that had escaped my lips, dripping its way down my chin and neck.

He finished ordering his drink from the bar and turned to look into my now burning red, embarrassed face. "I'm really good. Cheers, your looking good as always." He took a sip of his drink and gave me a panty-melting grin. "What's been happening with you?" His eyes were warm, and I was dissolving under his intense gaze. He smelled delicious and looked absolutely mouth-watering.

"Just work, not much else." I smiled up at him. I was only cleaning in the local school, but it was a job, and it paid the bills.

Logan is tall with mousy brown hair. A few long curls hung over his big, light, sea-blue bedroom eyes; so intense, I wanted to lick him instead of the drink dribbling down my face. His big eyes framed in thick dark lashes would make every female, and probably males, jealous as hell. His build is lean. His hard muscles covered in flawless, taut golden skin: a body made for sin. I was attracted to him instantly.

I haven't really changed much over the years. My brown hair now has blonde highlights and sits just past my shoulders. My skin is slightly tanned, my build small and petite. My best features are my dark blue eyes with crystal blue specks that sparkle in the sunlight. I am on the go every day, and a few visits to the gym every week, keeps my natural curves toned but feminine.

I am not the most confident person; that was beaten out of me by my ex-husband; the sadistic prick who tried to wear me down to make sure I never felt confident enough to survive without him.

"What's your tipple? Can I buy you a drink babe?"

I nearly choked on a breath. Can this really be happening? Is he asking if he can buy me a drink? Hell yes! He can buy me anything he likes looking like that!

"Vodka and diet coke, please, no ice. That's really kind of you, thank you."

I watched him as he ordered two Vodka and cokes, his T-shirt clinging to him in a way that hugged the hard lines of his long, solid muscles. I wanted to run my fingers over them to see how he felt.

He placed his hand into the small of my back and the warmth of his hand charged through my body spreading like fire through my veins.

"Oh my god."

I turned toward him and moved my hands to hold him in return, placing my hand on his amazing ass. I honestly could not help myself. That earned me another sexy-as-hell grin from him that made my knickers soaking wet.

As I stood there in his half-embrace, I noticed the glow of his golden skin. Even his jeans showcased his ass beautifully. He really was a striking package, in a manly way.

I felt his hands move slowly over my hips as I danced to the beat of the music. I turned into his stunningly large frame, his powerful arms wrapped around my middle as he moved his hands to cup my ass. Then he pressed his hips into me. I may have swooned.

Logan reached up and swept my hair to one side, exposing my skin there. I quivered in anticipation as I felt the heat of his breath blow against the sensitive skin at my neck, his fingers stroking along my shoulder blade. My body reacted, making my thighs clench tightly together.

I tilted my head slightly to the side in invitation; I was totally mesmerized by him like I had been hypnotised, completely lost in that moment. I couldn't help myself really. The only coherent thought I had at that moment was, 'God if I'm dreaming, please don't let me wake up. I don't want to miss this.'

His lips were firm but tender, moving slowly over my neck gently, sending a wave of heated pleasure through my whole body. A throbbing sensation hit me straight between my legs. I squeezed my thighs together again while my legs trembled and threatened to give way. He moved his hips in rhythm with mine as the sound of the music echoed in the background. It felt as though we are the only two people in the room, even though the club was, in fact, full of people having fun.

Turning me to him he leaned in and kissed me. I gripped his biceps and he groaned; a low, hungry growl emanated from his throat as his lips locked onto mine. He took my mouth prisoner, demanding I take everything he gave me. I couldn't breathe or speak to end the kiss.

Somewhere in the recesses of my brain, as I was locked in his embrace, I tried to fight against the urges that threatened to take over me. But being devoured like that rendered my involuntary reflexes useless. I couldn't resist as his tongue slipped into my mouth and found my own, each dueling for a deeper taste of the other. Wow, he could kiss.

As the song came to an end, we finally stopped to catch our breath. I looked up into his bright eyes burning into me; I had never seen an ocean blue so intense. It set off some primal response in me that made it impossible to say no to him. We found a table in the corner, out of the way of the busy bar, and we talked and talked about everything as if we had known each other for years. He was amazingly funny. I kind of struggled with his Scottish border accent at first. Being from Manchester, I am used to a different, very broad Scottish accent, but I got there in the end and I soon picked up his lingo.

I certainly had plenty of incentives to figure it out in a hurry. His voice was so husky and incredibly sexy; it only ramped up his pure male magnetism that seemed to sear into my bones, calling to me.

He told me stories about himself. He's a grafter and works on a lot of building sites when he's home. The rest of the time, he's in the special armed forces and is away a lot overseas, and he loves it. He loves working outdoors and getting his hands dirty. He is twenty-eight years old, my age, and pure and utter sex on ridiculously hot legs.

"We better get going after last orders, Dana. I'll walk you home."

I didn't want the night to end there. "Thanks, you're a star." I fought to pull my eyes away from his smoldering gaze. Butterflies started fluttering in my belly like they were having a party in there, the exquisite feeling heading straight to my pussy.

"Or do you want to come up to mine for a drink? If you fancy, it?" His gaze burns right through any power I might have had to resist this man. Oh my god, is he shitting me?

"Why not? Sounds like a plan." I was braver than I actually felt. I blushed brightly, trying to keep my legs from failing me, my typically clumsy countenance bad enough that it would have had me tripping over myself on a flat surface in a well-lit room. Add alcohol to the mix with my enchantment with this sex god and I almost lost any hope of avoiding falling on my ass. After the last round at the pub, Logan and I headed back to his place on foot. When we got to his house a few streets away, he put some music on and poured us both a Vodka and Coke.

"You want ice with that, gorgeous?" He leaned in and kissed me on lips so soft and firm, all I could do was shake my head no.

I gasped against his lips trying to catch my breath while his fingers ran through my hair, pulling at it softly, his lips so soft against mine the whole time. What a fucking amazing kisser. I pulled away slightly to break the magnetic pull he had on me.

"Slow down."

He didn't listen. He just pinned me against the wall and gripped my ass firmly in one hand, his other hand still in my hair.

"Why?"

He breathed into my lips, his eyes half-closed, hypnotizing me. I kissed him back, utterly losing any recollection of my protest moments before; I could have spontaneously combusted right there.

I lost all sense of propriety and started pulling at his T-shirt until I had it up and over his head. As it landed on the floor he grinned down at me, whipped my top over my head and threw it across the room. His lips were instantly back on my lips, my cheek, my ear, oh God, the ear. I was nearly out of my mind before he returned to my neck. With a swift unclipping of my bra, his hands were on me, kneading, grasping, hungry. I unbuttoned his jeans and I slid my hand down his boxers; my jeans were also gone in a flash.

Logan's tongue plunged deeply into my mouth; the passion devoured me, shock waves shooting through my whole body. His teeth nipped my bottom lip. His eyes burned wildly as I gasped into his mouth. Before I knew it, I was flat on my back staring up at his stunning chest, his mouth trailing kisses over my breast, circling my nipple with the tip of his tongue. My nipple immediately stood to attention.

My body was on fire; I wanted him so much. His kisses moved down to my stomach then to my clit. "Oh my god. What … are you doing to me?" I felt like I was going to explode at that very moment.

"Making you wet babe, and my name is Logan, not God." His voice breathed deliciously into my skin and under it, and I could hear the grin on his lips before they returned to mine.

His fingers slipped inside me; I was so wet. He fucked me with his fingers, sliding in and out of me in a delicious rhythm. My body begged for his as he loomed over me.

"Logan, I need you in me, now."

My words sounded shaky, my voice a husky out-of-breath tone as I breathed the words.

"You're so wet for me. How much do you want me, baby?"

I groaned. I couldn't bring myself to speak.

"How much do you want me, Dana?"

The more he demanded an answer, the more my body begged for him to be inside me.

I could feel myself pushing into him, my hips working into his, driving forward; my body took over, moving on its own. My mind told me to stop; the passion between us was a strong force that hit me like a ton of bricks.

"How can you make me feel so good? I've never been this turned on in my life," I whimpered and moaned in his ear. I never expected to feel that good. He slid between my legs and slammed his hard cock into me.

The orgasm built up inside me and almost instantly a deep, intense sensation took me to a place I had never been. This had never happened to me before No one had ever had such an affect on me. He buried his face between my breasts as he kept thrusting into me, kneading one breast with his hand as he kissed and sucked the other, circling his tongue over my nipple, fucking me like I had never been fucked before.

His pace became more frantic, as his own orgasm grew.

"Logan, please!"

My own orgasm hung by a thread as I begged him for release. I couldn't stand it. I had to let go. I screamed out his name as I came in an intense explosion, digging my fingernails into his back, squeezing him inside me, my walls clamping tight around him. The pain was exquisite. I had never felt that way before. Sweat poured off me. My body responded as I pushed towards him, shaking and quivering out of control.

My reaction to him triggered his own end, and he exploded into me, gasping my name. He pressed his lips to mine with hard, forceful kisses. He took my head in his hands and smiled down at me, his eyes warm and intense like liquid, trying to catch his breath.

"Dana, you're so beautiful. Are you ok?"

"Yes, I am more than ok. I think I just went to heaven," I laugh. I've never had an orgasm like that EVER in my life, I thought.

"Babe, I want more, so much more. I can take you back to heaven whenever you like." He grinned down at me so lovingly, giving me his beautiful seductive smile while softly rubbing his nose against mine and lightly pressing his forehead against my own.

Chapter Three

I wanted more of him. Damn, I wanted to devour him. We lay there, him still on top of me, for what felt like an age. His eyes burned with desire as I looked up at him drawn to his blazing blue eyes. We cuddled together, and fell asleep.

I woke up some time later to a huge, wet nose in my face. At first all I saw was black, then a light-brown face and big brown eyes. I jumped up when I realized something was sniffing at me; I nearly fall off the bed.

"What the hell is that?" I shrieked, having gotten the fright of my life.

"This is Holly. Isn't she stunning?" Logan said as he launched himself up out of bed.

"She's enormous!" I stared at the massive beautiful beast in front of me, her head as large as a dinner plate. She wagged her tail, obviously happy to see us. "A beautiful dog, but she's massive, more like a horse than a dog."

She looked like a big cuddly teddy bear. Logan had gotten her from a mate; she hadn't been treated very well and wasn't keen on men, but he had managed to bring her around, she accepted him. I watched him stroking the top of her head; she was a happy girl who just wanted her breakfast.

I looked up at Logan, and he grinned at me.

"What's funny?"

"She's a muckle softy. She won't hurt you."

"Muckle?" I looked at him confused, as I had never heard that word before, and I soon realised he meant big. I smiled at him. "I do love your accent, it's awesome."

After I had got over the shocking wake-up call from Logan's bullmastiff, I wanted to head downstairs and make a much-needed coffee. Logan then announced, as if he'd read my mind, that he was going to the kitchen to make coffee. I joined him after I got myself straightened out from our intense night. I watched him as he moved like a lion sauntering through his territory; he really was very fit and his body was so damn sexy. A tattoo splayed across his chest with the words, 'Who Dares Wins.'

His boxer shorts hung on his hips; he was just perfect in every way, like a male model. I got embarrassed when he caught me checking him out; my face heated up with the awkwardness.

I loved everything about him. Oh, those fucking eyes; they made him seem even sexier and real. But I already doubted myself - it would all be too good to be true; guys like him always are.

Thinking back about that time makes me smile as my soul remembers the love and intense passion we shared. We had our daughter, Amy, a year after we started dating. I fell pregnant with his child quickly but it felt so right; he felt so right for me. We fitted together; soul mates in the dark. He had his own darkness; he was recovering from an injury and was learning to come to terms with that. Also, not being able to help me when I had to run from my ex-husband made him feel inadequate; he didn't feel like a man. I had thought I was going to spend the rest of my life with him in Scotland, but things changed dramatically.

Amy is six years old now. It seems impossible to ever be a happy family, but I can dream about one. I have faith and I hold on to hope. I will always have a connection with him, an unbreakable bond. I hope I never lose it; I am missing him terribly.

I'm roused from my delicious daydream by the girls squealing with excitement. The girls love the hotel room.

"I can't wait until we get our own house mum!" Kayleigh is beautiful, small and petite, with big dark blue eyes and mousy brown hair. She is very confident, intelligent, funny, a force to be reckoned with. Kayleigh turns ten tomorrow. She is in year six at primary school and has made lots of new friends. Both of the girls like their new school, but desperately miss their old friends from Scotland. I'm so glad they can keep in touch by phone, text and Facebook.

We sit and talk about what we would do when we finally get our own house, how we are going to decorate it, and if we would be lucky enough to have a garden, what plants and flowers we would have, and, of course, a trampoline.

"I am having a princess bedroom all in pink," Amy beams her biggest smile at me. Amy loves princesses and Tinkerbell. She is just as lovely as her big sister, with blue eyes, long curly blonde hair and a slim build.

"One day we will be free to do as we please." I assure them. I send them off to take a bath before we go for our dinner.

I look at my phone and after unlocking the screen, I scroll through it. There are various texts from friends: Katy, Mandy, Rose, Vicky, and my mum, asking if we got here ok. I type out my message and send a mass text to everyone, letting them know we have arrived safe and sound, and to assure everyone that I hadn't got stuck on the train, broken my neck or lost the kids, or been killed along the way by some tragic mishap with my dodgy foot and my stupid clumsiness.

Beautiful place here, the girls adore it. Speak to you soon.

My thoughts are at home, thinking of my friends back at the refuge, wondering what they are all up to right now. I hope that my best mates, Katy and Rose, are okay as well as the rest of the girls; I miss them all. We live in close proximity in the refuge, and I'm so used to seeing them every day.

"This is weird. I've not even been here a day yet," I mumble to myself.

Katy's room is right next to ours. We each have our own battles, though they are all similar, running from crazy ass ex-husbands or boyfriends. My ex-husband, Ian, is a first class crazy ass mentalist and doesn't know when to give up. He got away with beating me for years. The police here in the UK are just starting to recognise domestic abuse as a crime, taking it more seriously.

Katy is the closest thing I have to a best friend. I met her in the refuge and haven't known her long, but we are like sisters living right next to each other under the same roof. She's only a few years older than me, and has natural blonde, platinum glossy hair, big green eyes, and freckles on her cheeks. Her slim build makes her look tall, although she's really only slightly taller than my five-foot-three inches.

Katy and the other girls from the refuge keep me going, keeping everything very focused and positive. They are always there for both me and my daughters and vice versa. I couldn't ask for a better support network, and it took us landing at the refuge to find that. Karma works in mysterious ways.

Surviving Him
from Dawn A Keane

I can still feel her soft body in my arms, her head on my chest and that sweet scent of hers filling my nostrils. We will always be unbreakable.

Dawn A Keane

Made in the USA
Charleston, SC
29 January 2016